Siren Songs from the Heart of Austin

Siren Songs
from
the Heart of Austin

Andrew Geyer

INK
BRUSH
PRESS

Temple, Texas

ISBN 978-0-9824405-5-1
Library of Congress Control Number
2009940562
Manufactured in the United States of America

Cover design- Lisa Craig
Cover photographs - Eric Beverly

Ink Brush Press
Temple, Texas
www.inkbrushpress.com

For Joshua, Caleb, and Savannah

of whom I am so very proud.

It is necessary to brave not only the siren's song, but also the dragons.

—Frithjof Shuon

If I can't love my baby, I can't live another day.

—Stevie Ray Vaughn

Acknowledgments

Grateful acknowledgment is made to the following publications, in which versions of these works of fiction previously appeared:

Amarillo Bay: "Love in Dead Languages"

Concho River Review: "An Epistle of My Heart"

descant: "Love Grudge"

Langdon Review of the Arts in Texas: "Pink Dolphin"

Nebo: "No Good in Goodbye"

New Texas 2001: "White Sands"

Pistolwhip: "Second Sight"

RE: Arts and Letters: "Fear Is a Lie Told in the Daytime"

Sojourn: A Journal of the Arts: "Tahini Is a Sesame Seed Paste"

Salt Fork Review: "Killing Kittens"

Taj Mahal Review: "I'm Connie Chung" and "White Rabbit"

I would like to thank Emily Geyer, Judy Geyer, Frank Geyer, Larry D. Thomas, Robert Flynn, Chuck Taylor, Jill Patterson, Doug Crowell, Stephen Graham Jones, Jeff Musgrave, Eric Beverly, Sherry Craven, and Jerry Craven, without whose guidance and generous assistance this story cycle would not exist.

Contents

Fear Is a Lie Told in the Daytime

I am the Prophet Mudcat. I am the one who sees. When the salamanders choose to speak, they speak through me.

As you are now, I once was. I lived my life in the daytime. At the surface. Gasping the thin air. Believing the evidence of my eyes. Accepting the lies of those who would keep us away from the truth that resides in the water.

Now I live my life in the absence of sun. In the moonlit depths of the water, the rightness of things can be ascertained by feel. I have beautiful catfish whiskers that I use to pick my way along the bottom, to navigate among the refracted stars.

I will give them to you.

As I am now, you will be. You will grow out new gills and remember how to breathe. You will glide in the liquefied light of the Milky Way.

This will be my gift to you.

Be not afraid. Fear is a lie told in the daytime to keep us apart in the dark. Put foil on your windows. Tape up sheets behind the foil and cram towels into the door-cracks. Close your eyes and open your mind. Your transition will be smooth and beautiful. Not at all like my own.

I was reborn in fire.

On July 4, 1997 at 11:30 p.m.—fifty years to the instant after Roswell—I was struck by lightning while swimming laps in Barton Springs. The bolt burned a hole in the back of my head and arced into the water. The pool went white-hot, my skull an electric pressure-cooker, the current an open circuit connecting my brain to every creature that scuttled or swam, from the uppermost reach of the springs to the Longhorn Dam. I saw through the eyes of carp and catfish. I hunched inside a crayfish shell. I took in water through bright red salamander gills.

I felt the salamanders take in air through me.

I felt them look through my eyes as we breathed together, felt their thoughts in my mind, felt my paradigm shift—Barton Springs / Austin / Texas / USA / Planet Earth / Spiral Arm / Milky Way. I knew the silence of the void was an illusion born from the deafness of mankind. I heard the X-ray screams of stars as they spiraled into black holes, and the white heat of my lightning was the same as their sound. All aglow with the salamander light I felt myself weighed, balanced, chosen. Their voices hissed into my mind like the radio whispers of quasars sent across a billion years and only just now received.

They said: At last . . . Our choice is Austin, Austin, Austin. Austin cubed. Austin to the hundredth power. Austin *ad infinitum*. The trendone is our medium. You will be our messenger. You will lead your world into a new age.

I said: Trendone?

They said: The trendone is what we make and what we are. The trendone is our instrument, the means of our conquest, the road to our victory here on Milky Way / Spiral Arm / Planet Earth. The people of your world are being kept in a coma. We will be their physicians. The trendone is their prescription. Think of yourself as their pharmacist. Wake them up.

I said: I'm not a druggist. I just got on at Dell.

They said: Do you not understand? Your life before is over. You have been chosen. You are the future of your world.

I said: Do amphibians not have ears? Dell! Profit sharing. Stock options. I just closed on a lakefront condo. Listen up! Future, no. Present, yes!

They said: Your present is face down in Barton Springs with its lungs full of water. But if that is what you wish to choose . . .

I felt the salamanders stop taking in air for me. I felt the water scald my face, felt my brain start to boil, felt my lungs fill with hot lead.

I said: Future, yes! Future, yes!

I awoke to the smell of burnt hair and the sound of voices. The pain in my head paralyzed my whole body. Someone had pulled me from the pool, CPR'ed me back to life—it turns out I was dead almost five minutes—and placed a 911 call. In the ambulance I dreamed I was Odysseus starting out on a journey home to places I never imagined. Islands in an interstellar ocean. The myriad planets of the Milky Way. I saw towers made of light that soared higher than mountains. I saw cities at the bottom of seas. I saw ancient civilizations bound together by saucer-shaped ships sailing X-ray tradewinds born from the death throes of suns. I heard the salamander voices wild and sweet as the winedark void hiss across my mind, promising all this and more for dumb old aggressive bipedal mankind.

The hospital was a weird déjà vu nightmare of white sheets, antiseptics, emergency surgery, pain. Doctors talking to Mother, Mother talking to doctors. Blood and urine tests. CAT scans. More surgery. The inside of my head on fire. Specialists. More CAT scans. More specialists. Even more CAT scans. Mother talking to doctors, doctors talking to specialists, specialists talking to specialists—and only the salamanders talking to me.

They said: Roswell . . .

The doctors said: Brain trauma.

The specialists said: Permanent tissue loss. Neurons don't regenerate.

Mother said prayers.

The salamanders said: Upgrading chromosomal systems. Please wait.

The doctors said: Brain cancer.

The specialists said: Accelerated cell growth. Altered DNA.

Mother said more prayers.

I said: Salamanders! What are you doing to me?

The salamanders said: Downloading communications software. Please wait.

3

I said: Are you God?

The salamanders said: We are social workers. At coordinates Milky Way / Spiral Arm / Planet Earth / USA / New Mexico / Roswell / 1947 / July 4 / 11:30 p.m., a saucer ship on a mission of peace was shot down by the paranoid Air Force of the USA.

I said: Peace? A while ago, you were talking about conquest.

They said: A metaphor. Our peace mission came in response to your first atomic blasts. We believed they were a cosmic smoke signal, an aboriginal attempt to establish trade. So we sent an ambassador with a few technological trinkets, to see what you had to exchange. He flew toward Los Alamos, which we believed to be your communications center, with open arms and lowered shields—only to be blasted out of the sky over Roswell. You impounded our saucer ship, dissected our ambassador, reverse-engineered our technology, and infringed our patent rights. As a result, a second mission was sent. This mission. Our mission.

I said: This is the conquest part, right?

The salamanders said: Actually, we've ruled out an invasion *per se* and decided to stage a love-in. But back to the briefing. We salamanders—there are others in pools throughout the Southwest—were sent here to evaluate your species. Specifically, we were to choose one of three options: annihilation, enslavement, or re-education. After fifty years of study, we reached our conclusion: your species is basically good-hearted, but critically unhip.

I said: You said something about a love-in?

They said: Have you ever asked yourself what it is about bipeds that causes them to spend so much time fretting about fornication and so little time engaged in the act of love?

I said: To be honest, I'm always too busy thinking about getting laid.

They said: Precisely. The total separation of your species from a marine environment has caused a breakdown in chemical communications between the sexes. The result? Anomie. Nihilism. Naked aggression. Hence, our decision—and your mission—the partial reintroduction of said species to hydrous respiration and the restoration of pheromone-based relations.

I said: My mission is what?

They said: To make ready for the Age of Aquarius and pave the way for a new society of the cosmically hip.

I said: The love-in?

The salamanders said: Run Roswell.exe.

I felt a wave of white heat sweep across my body like sheet lightning and set ablaze the night sky of my mind. It was as though all my cells had been injected with acid. Then everything was suddenly so Austin. So alternative. So live from the culture desk. I felt an uncontrollable urge to quit my job, get tattooed, gather circles in Pease Park and pound percussion instruments, play frisbee golf. I felt all my violent impulses go up in a puff of what smelled like pot smoke.

I said: THC?

The salamanders said: Trendone.

And so the process went on. Trendiculation. Transformation. I began to feel more in touch with my body. I felt my brain cells regenerated, my ganglia re-networked, my damaged synapses reformed and re-fired. I felt bone, muscle, skin, regrowing. I even grew out a new head of hair. The whole time I heard the salamanders whispering, downloading a steady stream of data onto my newly upgraded hard-drive.

I said: Explain.

The salamanders said: The trendone is a super sex hormone we secrete from glands at the base of our tails. You will harvest the trendone from the waters of Barton Springs and distribute it into the bodily fluids of your fellow Austinites—who, in the course of their impressively prolific coital communications, will spread the trendone far and wide. Austin will become the hub in a world wheel of peace and prosperity—a kinder, gentler societal vehicle driven by an interstellar perspective as cool as absolute zero and fueled by trade with alien beings . . .

Finally the fire in my head began to die a little, and the salamander voices started to fade. I felt as though I had swum an entire ocean, been burnt black by sun, pummeled blue by wind and wave. But at the same time I had a feeling of being reborn, of having reached the farthest shore. Black and blue, pink and new, I opened my eyes on a hospital room.

I squinted into the glare of fluorescent lights glinting off stainless steel instruments. I made out chrome-and-white machines with digital read-outs, most of which seemed to be hooked up to me. I saw a gaunt, gum-smacking angel perched at my bedside; felt my mother's hand warm against mine. I looked up into Mother's face and squeezed her fingers.

I said: Roswell . . .

Mother said: It's a miracle! Sweet Jesus! My baby boy is awake! The doctors said you'd never come out of that coma. And the specialists . . . Well, never mind what they said. I've been at your bedside three days. Speak to me, baby! Show Mother you're not brain-dead.

I said: It's you that's brain-dead, Mother. And the US Air Force's fairy tale about Roswell is what's keeping you comatose.

She said: Stop insulting your mother with conspiracy theories, and say a prayer of thanksgiving for this miracle of God.

I said: It wasn't God. It was alien social workers living in Barton Springs. I've had an upgrade, Mother. They downloaded their database onto my hard-drive. Deny, deny, deny! The Air Force's spin on Roswell is a poison apple of paranoia cooked up in a witch's brew of lies. We're a planet of Sleeping Beauties, Mother! To wake up from our coma, we have to open our eyes.

I saw Mother lean closer, saw her eyes go wider the deeper they looked into mine. I felt her breath on my face as she bent over the bed, smelled smacked-to-death

Dentyne, the three-day prayer fuzz on her tongue. Then I heard her shriek, saw her leap back like I was some kind of monster. I caught the low-heeled clack of sensible shoes as she screamed her way out of the room.

She said: It's a reptile! Jesus Lizard! My baby boy has reptile eyes! It's a clear-cut case of medical malpractice! Lizard eyes! Lizard eyes!

I said: Oh no.

The salamanders said: They are much more like catfish eyes, actually. And quite beguiling. The females of your species will soon be running wild.

I said: My mother is running wild right now.

They said: Put your faith in pharmaceuticals. A little dose of trendone in the water supply, a little time, and these new hybridized catfish eyes will be all the rage.

I said: I'm a hybrid catfish?

They said: The ostariophysians are a truly superior species. Catfish cooperate through chemical communications, form breeding pairs, protect their eggs and newly-hatched young—

I said: A hybrid egg-protecting catfish?

They said: It's more than your mother will do.

Just then Mother lurched into the room dragging a doctor under one arm and a nurse across her back. It took the doctor a surprising amount of time and strength to wrench himself away from my mother. Then while the nurse worked Mother into a modified half-nelson, he locked a hand across my face, pulled my eyelids back, and blazed a flashlight like a blowtorch onto my optic nerve.

I said: Aaahhh!!!

Dr. Face-Lock said: These are not lizard eyes, ma'am. As I told you in the nurse's station, that would imply a greater aberration than actually exists. Come on up and look. Come on.

Mother said: All right.

Nurse Half-Nelson let my mother edge closer.

Dr. Face-Lock said: Lizards have a very primitive kind of eye called a median, or pineal, eye. The pineal eye

7

is placed at the top of the head. As you can see, your son's eyes are right where they ought to be in a more advanced vertebrate. His eyes are lateral, just like yours and mine.

Mother said: But they're gold! My baby's eyes are supposed to be blue. And they move funny. See?

Dr. Face-Lock said: I don't know about the color, but you're right about the movement. There is something odd about the function of the lens. Hmm. His eyes have a spherical lens that moves to focus within the eyeball. They look almost like—

Nurse Half-Nelson said: Fish! Not lizard, catfish! My first ex ran a catfish farm. He must've filleted a million branches of this freak's family tree.

The salamanders said: Savages!

Mother fainted dead away. While Nurse Half-Nelson got busy reviving my mother, Dr. Face-Lock shifted his grip, pushed a bright red button over the bed, and turned his light on my neck. Then people in surgical scrubs started streaming in, shouting back and forth across my hospital bed about how best to physically document the freak transformation of me.

The specialists said: Exploratory brain surgery! Collect neuron samples!

The doctors said: Remove his gills!

Nurse Half-Nelson said: First you hook 'em, then you gig 'em!

Dr. Face-Lock called for orderlies and a crash cart, while the rest of them eyed me like a catfish buffet. Finally the whole bunch—doctors, specialists, nurses, and my newly-revived mother—came at me like starving cannibals with a hypo the size of a spear.

The salamanders said: Defend your life!

I said: Stop! I refuse further treatment of any kind. Violate my person, and every last one of you loses the right to practice medicine in this state.

They halted to a man. Only Mother kept coming, dragging Nurse Half-Nelson along until she reapplied her hold. Dr. Face-Lock let go his grip, put on his best bedside manner, unbuckled my restraints. Then he unhooked all my tubes and wires, and telephoned the desk nurse to walk release papers up.

Mother said: But he's deformed!

Dr. Face-Lock said: He's a mutant, ma'am. But as long as he's conscious, he's got the same rights as you or me.

I struggled out of bed, naked and unsteady, and saw Mother hide her face. When my feet hit the floor, I discovered my toes were webbed, which knocked my balance out of whack. I stumbled into a set of scrubs, scribbled my name on the death-waver, staggered to the door. Then it was down the hall, through the lobby, out onto Fifteenth Street in the dark—where I stopped to spew the contents of my belly onto my bare and newly-finned feet.

The salamanders said: Are you unwell?

I said: The whole world reeks of garbage and car exhaust, and I can smell with my mouth.

They said: You need to initiate hydrous respiration to make the transformation complete. Head for Town Lake. There is no need to run, but walk quickly. We do not have much time.

As I staggered downhill toward I-35, I realized I could see in the dark. I saw better at midnight as a hybrid fish than at noon as a human being. I could hear better, too. Even with all the traffic noise from the freeway, I made out footsteps a hundred yards back. I looked behind me as I turned to walk along the frontage road and saw five men in surgical scrubs moving up fast.

I said: Some of those doctors are following me.

The salamanders said: Those men are not doctors. Run!

The fourteen blocks between me and Town Lake seemed to stretch into fourteen miles. I was off-balance, gangly, running on webbed feet for the first time in my life, gasping for air through a mouth that was also a nose. Behind me, the men who weren't doctors kept gaining ground. My new improved ears couldn't help but pick up their athletic breaths closing in on my own ragged wheeze.

I said: Those men must be trained runners!

The salamanders said: Those men are Air Force assassins. If they overtake you, they will harvest your body parts.

They were right on top of me by the time I finally reached the park. The feel of carpet grass was like cool aloe vera on my battered feet, and I heard the footsteps grind to a stop. I was beginning to think I might make it when projectiles started to hurtle past me at sickening speeds, followed closely by pistol reports.

The salamanders said: Dive!

I leaped into space. For a long moment I hung suspended in a swarm of bullets that buzzed around my body like bees boiling off a hive. Then I broke the surface of the water and clawed my way along the bottom, wondering how long I could stay down.

I said: What now, geniuses?

The salamanders said: Take a breath, and take a new name.

The surface of the lake glistened above me like the skin of a living sky. I took a breath. Another. I felt a wild euphoria set in. The heavens floated in the water around me as the walls of the space-time continuum dissolved in liquid starshine. I swam the Milky Way in Town Lake, caught the whisper of cosmic waves upon Auditorium Shores, heard the hiss of gas clouds raining the stuff of new stars on the statue of Stevie Ray Vaughn. On the bottom below me, I watched the real Roswell replayed. I saw a saucer ship shot down in the high desert, witnessed alien autopsies, viewed the top-secret hangar where a new generation of stealth aircraft was reverse-engineered, along with the Internet and the desktop PC—a kind of 5-D docudrama among the beer bottles and mud.

I said: I will be Mudcat.

The salamanders said: Follow us, Prophet Mudcat, and make fish out of men . . .

And so I sing you this siren song, my soon-to-be brothers and sisters, as I start my nightly rounds. I swim laps in Barton Springs while the western sky fades pastel. I glean trendone in the gloaming from beneath bright red salamander tails. Then I head off to work the late shift at the water treatment plant.

It is peaceful here, so secluded, among the throb of the machines—only me, my mop, a bucketful of alien sex hormones, and the Austin water supply. Brothers and sisters, you have only to drink to receive.

Every morning at dawn the dayshift manager scowls his way in. Tense already, carnally constipated, sexually dispossessed, he asks me curtly how it went last night.

He says: What the hell went wrong?

I smile. I hand him a brimming cupful from the cooler, full of the fruits of last night's work.

I say: Relax. Drink the water.

Killing Kittens

The dream has come to me every night this week. In it, I am red and hard-shelled—a lobster. I lie at the bottom of a pile of lobsters, fighting for air in an un-aerated tank, struggling to free my claws from the wire bands that clamp them shut. I am helpless before the hand that dips into the tank again and again, taking us one by one, never to return. Then I feel the hand close on my carapace, feel myself lifted—

"Joe? Wake up."

"Oh . . . " I say, still dreaming that I am a lobster.

"Wake up, Joe. Wake—"

"Oh . . . no," I say, still a lobster with my claws wired closed.

"—up! Get up! Joe!" Elizabeth's whisper is a frothy pot-boil I feel myself tossed into. "Get up and turn off that alarm before it wakes the baby!"

"Oh . . . kay," I say, simmering awake. 4:56 a.m. I am eleven minutes late already. And soaked in sweat all down my right side. Wait a minute. Why only on one side? "Oh . . . God! Oh God!"

"What's the matter?"

"The baby's diaper leaked in the bed again."

"Shh. I'll get the diaper," Elizabeth says. "You get to work. You're twelve minutes late for Number Two."

Number Two means working weekends, waiting tables at Aqua Vitae Café. Down the hall half-coated in number one, I half-hop, half-stagger. In the nightlight, my glow-in-the-dark Aqua Vitae Café T-shirt reels like a drunken moon. I kick baby toys, cat toys, kittens from my path to reach the kitchen, the coffee pot, and start my twenty-sixth day in a row of iron man triathlon labor—one newborn baby, two jobs, three golden showers—on maybe four total nights of sleep.

"Aqua Vitae Café!" someone shouts into my ear.

"Home of the twenty-four hour pterodactyl. Glow-in-the-dark latenite land. Birthplace of the Mother's Day Lobster Brunch. This is Bruno! How may I help you?"

"This is Joe," I say into the receiver. I do not remember dialing the phone. I don't remember picking it up.

"Joe! You mean Joe Teacher Joe, or Joe the Lead Singer of the Pixels Joe? You don't sound much like Joe Manager Joe, and anyway, Joe Manager Joe's right here!"

"This is the Joe who was supposed to be there thirteen minutes ago, to set up for lobster brunch."

"Joe Teacher Joe! Hey! What's the Quote of the Day?" Bruno says at the top of his lungs, a kind of manic monotone.

"*Diarrhea oris*," I say, "is the Quote of the Day."

"Wow! Hey, what's that mean?"

"*Happy Mother's Day* in Latin."

"Well, *diarrhea oris*, Joe Teacher Joe! You're fourteen minutes late, man. We're slammed! Joe Manager Joe says he's gonna tear you a new one. Let me let you talk to—"

"No! Bruno! Take a message. Tell Manager Joe my baby peed on me. Got it? Baby pee. On me."

"Hey, Joe Manager Joe! *Diarrhea oris*, man. Joe Teacher Joe says he's got—"

"Half an hour!" Manager Joe snarls into the phone, having apparently manhandled it away from Bruno. "You hear me, smart boy? Your dead-language-teaching ass had best be slinging lobster by half past five."

Autopilot. One. Hang up on Manager Joe.

Two. Take the phone off the hook.

Three. Lightspeed morning routine. I feed and water kittens, scoop out the litterbox—which some dormant corner of my brain registers is strangely empty—then gather up the take-out trash, refill my coffee, and head into the living room to catch the top end of CNN Headline News.

Four. My hard-won respite is overwhelmed by an

eruption of kitten crap.

Five. There shouldn't be a four. But the stench of kitty diarrhea comes bubbling up, hot and fetid as the terrible tapioca between my toes. The delicate bouquet of coffee and sound-byte reporting goes sour with bile, and I find myself thinking of killing kittens.

It is not an idle fancy. It's more like one of the road rage replays we all run through in our heads to blow off steam—except that it involves the dismembered bodies of two half-siamese, half-himalayan kittens instead of the smoking remains of an SUV. I feel it almost working, feel my fingers unclenching from the River City Community College coffee cup I got from the Dean of the Humanities Department in lieu of a living wage. Then I see piles of kitten poop on the baby's books. I see yellow kitty diarrhea smeared across the faces of the Teletubbies, the Teeny Tiny Monster, Winnie the Pooh.

And I feel myself start to flip out for real.

It's like watching me through backwards binoculars. I see myself catch hold of Mischief, the dominant kitten—her white fluffy face buried in cat chow—and start smacking the back of her head. I hardly feel her claws shred the flesh on my forearms as I roll her in feces and drop-kick her out the front door. I see myself run down Blue—runt imitator of her older sister—and do the same to her. Then I see that the entire top layer of baby books, at five to fifteen dollars a pop, is soaked through with kitten filth.

And I find myself in the hall closet, reaching for the shotgun.

The feel of the 12-gauge in my hands is as cold and deadly as my intentions. I break open the double barrels, catch the gleam of brass-butted shells, snap the shotgun shut, and head for the front porch to wake the neighborhood with two staccato blasts. Then the same dormant corner of my brain that noticed the empty litter box registers the gaping hole this will blow in the thin-stretched fabric of my marriage—the new baby, the jobs, the debt, the sleepless nights all pulling Elizabeth and me apart at the seams.

And I force myself, shotgun in hand, to phone my mother.

"I'm about to kill the kittens," I hear myself say. "I'm holding a shotgun right now, about to introduce brains to bungholes. But the way things have been going lately, I'm afraid Elizabeth will leave."

"Is that your father's double-barrel 12-gauge?" the old woman counters, calm as the lowing of the cattle grazing outside her kitchen window. At 5:05 a.m. she and the old man are on their second cup of coffee. "He's been looking for that gun."

"He gave it to me," I say, gripping it tighter—but playing her game, feeling the 162 miles between hell in South Austin and home in Southwest Texas melt into the sound of my father bellowing about the shotgun.

"That's not what he says. Anyway, I thought y'all had agreed to get rid of that older cat. The one that keeps peeing in the plants and pooping on your students' papers."

"Mischief. Yes ma'am. But Elizabeth wouldn't let me go through with it." I remember the confrontation: the soft-hearted Carolina city girl versus the hard-nosed Southwest Texan who grew up raising cattle for slaughter. "She held the evil bitch on her lap and cried about being its mommy."

"Joey? Your father says to put down his shotgun. Put the gun down right now, baby, or I'm hanging up."

I lean the shotgun in a corner and stand there beside it like a three-year-old being made to take a time out. "Please don't hang up. Dad can have the gun. Just help me figure out what to do."

"You take those kitties for a ride," the old woman says, the sound of her voice steady as the Southwest Texas sun at noon. "Say they wandered off into the brush after a cottontail."

"But we live in the city, Mother. There's no brush

15

around. And no cottontails, either."

"Then say they got stolen off the porch."

"Stolen? That's one I hadn't thought of."

"A little white lie can work miracles. I wonder how many of your old animals got stolen off the porch, or wandered off after cottontails? Let's see now, there must have been . . . one, two, three—"

"Wait a minute. Those were my pets!"

"Aren't those kitties the baby's pets?"

"But . . . Mother, you didn't dump off old Collie, did you? Not Collie," I say, remembering the black-and-white border collie with a sweet tooth that I grew up sharing ice cream and cookies with on the sly. "She really did get stolen off the porch."

"Well, no . . . but we didn't dump her, either. Your father hit old Collie with the hay truck one morning. Broke both her back legs. I believe he shot her with that same double-barrel 12-gauge."

"With my own gun? I had that dog thirteen years! She was as much a part of the family as you or me."

"No, son. She was an animal. And sometimes animals have to be put down. You used to understand that."

"My God," I say. "You're right. Happy Mother's Day."

I hang up the phone and walk out the front door in tears for a dog that's been dead more than a decade. I sit down and pull on the crusty Aqua Vitae Café workshoes that Elizabeth won't let me bring in the house—so coated in eggs and bacon grease and the rarified remains of spoiled milk that I have to hang them from the rafters to keep the neighborhood animals from carrying them away. Purring like an idiot, little Blue rubs her feces-matted fur against my leg in a belated apology. Her renegade sister squats in a potted plant, taking revenge. But my mind is 162 miles southwest and more than ten years distant, standing in my father's boots, pointing his 12-gauge shotgun down at a broken-legged border collie—and knowing I can't pull the trigger.

I get into the car and head for Aqua Vitae Café, having decided the kittens can stay. The feel of defeat at the hands of my soft-hearted girl from Carolina is not half as heavy as the filth-encrusted shoes on my feet. But heaviest of all, as I blow through stop sign after stop sign, praying none of my RCCC colleagues brings in their mothers for lobster and eggs, is the question of how the distance between myself here and now and that hard-nosed Southwest Texan became so much more than a measure of miles.

An Epistle of My Heart

Yesterday, on the evening news, Connie Chung looked me straight in the eye and said the fires in Guatemala posed no threat to American lives. The Indians had set the fires themselves, she said, believing the rains would come as they had always come, and the flames would be quenched to make way for fields. But El Niño had come instead, and the rain forest still burned. The tight lines of Connie's face softened a second—as though she could see the footage of thatch huts ablaze on the blue screen behind her—then it was back to straight-in-the-eye Chung, a tough cookie. This was the source of the pall of smoke that hung in the air over Texas, she said, and on the blue screen, I saw the sun burn pale as the moon, like it had burned in the haze over Austin all day.

"*Pobrecitos*," my grandfather said, eyeing Connie. "Harry spent a good bit of time there when he was in the Peace Corps, you know. Twenty months in Guatemala, teaching—"

"Teaching the Indians how *not* to farm," I broke in. "Ha, ha. The first twenty thousand times I heard that, I almost laughed."

"Perhaps the mature and sensitive Ms. Chung would appreciate Harry's Latin America experiences more than a certain ironical thirteen-year-old *presentadora* wannabe," he said, then I saw his eyes mist over. "She seemed about to burst into tears a second ago, looking at those Indians."

"Crocodile tears, Harry. That's a blank screen behind her. The only thing Connie sees is the tele-prompter. What a pro."

"There is a frozen sea inside her," Harry said, and wiped his eyes. "I must send her an epistle of my heart."

My grandfather's name is Harry. He's the oldest hippy left alive, and he's been living in Austin since before forever. The word he calls himself by is even old. *Beatnik*.

Who ever heard of that? Harry says Beatniks were hippies before hippies were hippies, which makes about as much sense as anything else Harry says. Fifties hippies must have been dinosaurs. I mean, scratchy vinyl albums? Black and white TV? Lethy calls Harry a *tejano* tyrannosaurus with a white braid and beard.

Maybe she's right. He is a little bossy. Okay, maybe a lot. But the thing about Harry is that he really cares about people. He's always coming up with these crazy ideas to improve lives. Edible appliances. Streets that glow in the dark. A collection of poems he calls *epístolas del corazón*. Letters from the heart. Harry lives his life like a letter from the heart, an epic poem to lost causes, giving loads of time and money and love to people who never had a chance.

Today's cause is my mother and me. Harry is trying to keep us away from Eeyore's Birthday Party, because he's worried about junk. *Junk* is what Harry calls drugs—heroin mostly; but when Harry gets wound up, *junk* can mean anything from pot to mushrooms to glue. He says that at Eeyore's Birthday Party there will be more junk than cotton candy and more junkies than kids. When I ask why he thinks so, Harry gets on this high horse about his junkie past, which means the conversation is over. Like my dad is always trying to tell Harry, a conversation cannot consist of one man talking.

But my grandfather is a non-practicing heroin addict—not cured, he says, but clean—and he's got that ex-junkie tough-love thing working like an ex-smoker times ten. Harry calls junk a chronic disease. He says where the junk goes once it gets in you, the cure can't reach. My dad keeps trying to tell Harry that he, Daddy, is cured. But Harry says that's just because Daddy's in prison and wants him, Harry, to "pound out to my *compadres* on the parole board yet another *epístola del corazón*." Harry must have started getting ready to keep us away from Eeyore's Birthday Party before dawn.

I awake to silence. The sun oozes like a blob in a

lava lamp up into the attic window; and for the first time I can remember, I am alone. Harry is not here—not hunched over his desk in the corner six feet from the side of my bed, pounding away at his epistles like he's pounded away at that crazy old manual typewriter every waking day of my life, his long white hair swinging wild and his beard getting stuck in the keys. This morning there is only silence, the smell of smoke, the lava lamp sun in the window; and it comes to me, all of a sudden, that the world is on fire.

"Harry!" I leap out of bed and yell. "The world is on fire!" Down the stairs, through the kitchen that is empty except for the blood red light of the sun, I run screaming. "The world is on fire! We're all going to burn!"

"No, *Cacahuete!*" Harry says as I burst out onto the porch and burrow into his beard. "*Cacahuetita,* no. It's okay, my little Peanut. It's not the world burning, but only those Indians in Guatemala. *Pobrecitos.*"

"How do you know?"

"Why, Connie Chung herself said so. Remember?"

At the mention of my idol, I pull back a little from the prickly warmth of my grandfather's chest. "No threat to American lives?" I ask.

"That's Harry's Peanut. Now go put on some clothes. It's time to set the yard up for the volleyball."

By the time I get back outside, Harry has the net up and is laying chalk lines in the grass—white shores of a green island safe from junk and junkies, from the sky turned to smoke, and from the fiery red horse of a sun like in the Bible. Me, he puts to work making signs. On one, he has me paint GAME IN PROGRESS; and on one, NEW GAME, stapling the posterboard onto wooden stakes that I set aside. On the third sign, Harry himself paints: NO JUNK ALLOWED. When he's done, Harry tacks the NO JUNK ALLOWED sign onto the porch. Then he settles into his rocking chair, twisting braids in his beard and drinking cup after cup of Aqua Vitae Blend coffee brewed from fresh-ground beans that he buys by the bag at a restaurant on Congress Avenue.

But it isn't long before the sound of electric guitars cranks up down at Eeyore's Birthday Party, drifting the block and a half from Pease Park onto our porch. It's not a real birthday party, of course, since it is based on a fictional character—a junk orgy for a make-believe jackass, Harry says—but they celebrate it anyway every spring and they have a *piñata*. Cars start pulling up along the front curb. The first clumps of party-goers pile out into the street, long-haired stumblers already smoking reefer as they stagger out of their cars among little girls and boys who run in circles and carry rainbow-colored balloons that bob on the marijuana breeze.

"Whenever you're ready, *Cacahuetita!*" Harry calls out.

I plant the NEW GAME sign. Harry lobs the ball inside the chalk lines. We start to volley. Pretty soon, it's Harry and me and a couple of other people. Then a couple more; and before long, Harry is splitting us up into teams. He uproots the NEW GAME sign and plants the sign that says GAME IN PROGRESS. Then he climbs up onto the porch and yells, "Play ball!"

And we do. Harry plays referee. As an umpire he is very much the *tejano* tyrannosaurus of Lethy's nickname. As long as things run smoothly, Harry remains *mi abuelo latino*, my Latino grandfather smiling but firm, waving encouragement as he yells, "Out of bounds!" But if anybody dares to argue a call, he becomes the tyrannosaur—turning around and roaring insults at the house until the complainer sees the error of his angry ways and remembers that it's just a game.

We play best-of-three's. Every time a series ends, another bunch of volleyballers heads downhill to become one with Eeyore; and I'm stuck here in the yard with Lethy and Harry, and the sun gone pale in a sky that smells like ashes. Lethy managed to drag her ass out of the house around midmorning—anyway, the half that always seems to hang out of her shorts—and after sitting

21

on the porch for awhile yelling at Harry, she got into the game. Lethy is short for Leticia. She's always saying, "Call me Mommy!" But I say I won't until she plays the part. Right now she can hardly play volleyball, and it isn't just because she's too busy making goo-goo eyes at everything in pants. Even though she's young, not yet thirty, the junk makes her move like an old woman.

Lethy isn't clean.

Between series, she slips into the house to take sneak-a-toke hits and rinse her eyes with Visene. She keeps a stash behind the false back of her panty drawer. And although I know this is forbidden—that staying clean is a condition of Lethy's living in the house—I find myself keeping quiet. I still love her, I guess, even though she screws around on Daddy; and I don't want Harry to kick her out.

Lunch is bean and potato tacos with Harry's home-grown garlic and onions and fiery red *chilipitins* stir-fried in. Harry and me eat in the kitchen like always, three tacos apiece so hot they make our eyeballs sweat. Afterwards, he fixes Lethy a plate that he sets aside. Lethy refuses to eat with Harry, even though he lets her live here free.

I'm scraping the crust off Harry's big cast-iron skillet when I hear the drum circle start up at Pease Park. The first hesitant *tump-tump-tump* like a faucet dripping swells into a drumbeat flood—ten, twenty, fifty hands funking out these crazy Calypso-meltdown rhythms—and I feel my heart accelerate until I know it must explode. My hands churn hot dishwater. My bare feet hiss across the kitchen tile. My bellybutton scratches the formica counter like a matchtip.

The rhythm boosts me out onto the porch like I'm riding a rocket. "Please, Harry?" I say, soap suds flying from my fingers, my bare toes wriggling at astronomical speeds. "Please can't I go to Eeyore's?"

"Ohhh . . ." Harry groans.

"Just until the next band! Come on! You know how

much I love you, Harry. If you let me go, I'll love you even more. Please please please—"

"*Cacahuetita*," he groans, "Harry loves you more than living. But he's beginning to get a cold, cold feeling about today." Harry gets this feeling sometimes like there's ice in his bowels; and every time he does, something terrible happens—the colder the feeling, the worse the bad thing that comes. He could've farted a blizzard, he always says, the night the cops came and took my dad. "Where the hell is your mother? Go find your mother, Peanut. Go right now! Harry feels like he's about to shit liquid nitrogen."

I ferret out Lethy in a hedge of box elders on the far side of the house. Her rolled-up pink tube-top coils like a snake around her neck. Her zipper is down, and one of the guys she's been making eyes at all morning has a hand inside her canary yellow shorts. With the other hand, just as I peek through the deep green screen of leaves, he slips a tiny paper square into her mouth.

"What the hell is that?" I ask, knowing the answer is LSD, but not wanting to think about what the other hand is doing. "Did you just drop acid, Lethy?"

The guy jerks his head around at me. "Ahh . . ." His voice is thick, his eyes screwed up, his hair *pachuco* clipped. The arm not inside my mother's shorts is gang-tattooed. "*Fresas frescas*," he says. Fresh strawberries. As he smacks his lips, I see a Robert Deniro mole on his cheek. Then I realize that he's staring at my breasts. "I've got enough for both of you. *¿Qué dices, chiquitita?*"

For a while, I say nothing at all. It's like my brain controls are frozen. I remember Harry telling me over and over that junk makes girls stupid and slutty and will give them pimples. I know in my heart that I don't want to drop acid. But the thought grinding like a glacier through the icefield in my head is that I tried mushrooms once, and am still a virgin. Harry is all the time saying I'm smart—*precoz*, he says—and I don't think a quarter-bag of shrooms can change that. But I worry sometimes. What I

23

want more than anything is to be like Connie Chung—not only beautiful, but brilliant; the anchor; always in control, no matter what goes on behind me. How can I be the anchor if I'm covered with zits?

"Get your hand out of my mother's pants!" I say at last.

"Come a little closer," Mr. Gangster says, "and I'll put my hand in yours."

"What the hell do you want with that *niña*," Lethy says, "when you've got *esta mujer*?" She sticks her tongue into his ear and wriggles her hips in a way that makes me ashamed to be alive.

I feel the ice in my brain turn to slush. Then the box elders go blurry, and I find myself wishing that the world really would end in fire so I could watch Lethy and Mr. Gangster burn to cinders. But in the here and now of Austin, Texas, not even my tears are scalding. I slog away into the icemelt of my world, not caring where I'm going.

Somehow, my feet find their way back to Harry.

"Did you see your mother?" he asks gently.

"Lethy's lying down in the shade."

Harry puts his arms around me. For a long time, we just hold each other; and the only sound in the world is my grandfather's heart. "Maybe it's time we took a break from the volleyball," he says at last. "Go get the camera, *Cacahuetita*. We'll tape a letter to your dad."

Harry sets up the camcorder on a tripod next to his rocking chair; and as the red light comes on, I feel the knot in my belly start to loosen. Daddy has been in prison for three years now—not just some county jail or white-collar tax lock-up, but in the Ellis Unit at the Texas State Pen. Hard time, Harry says, for a hard crime. Dealing tainted heroin. Someone's thirteen-year-old daughter, Harry says, died.

But Daddy says that's all finished. He says that he's cured. He says that he wants us to start our lives over again, together.

Lethy says that Daddy will never get out. But I

don't believe it, and I send him these video love letters so he will take heart. Harry says that writing the letters would be better for my schoolwork, and would keep me from spending so much time in front of the TV. I tell him that making the videos is good practice for my future career as the next Connie Chung. But the truth is that when I'm looking into the red light, nothing and no one else can touch me—and the only thing I cry is crocodile tears.

I fill Daddy in on what's been happening the last couple of weeks in Austin, about it being Eeyore's Birthday Party today, and about the volleyball. By the time I've covered the series scores, I'm almost myself again. Another crowd has gathered around the net, and I tell Harry that a little live footage would be a great way to cap off the tape. Harry agrees, and says he will shoot it.

He even lets me make the teams. I count out, "One, two, one, two," sending every other player to opposite sides of the net. Lethy and Mr. Gangster come walking out of the box elders just as I'm finishing up. But this time, with the red light on and the camcorder rolling, my brain stays frost-free. At least they're not holding hands, I think to myself. Then I send them both to the same side of the net as the camera. That way, my dad won't have to look their sorry asses in the face.

"Play ball!" I yell.

And we do. It turns out that Mr. Gangster has a temper, and he's a loudmouth to boot. Pretty soon he's stirring up trouble with one of the guys on my team. My guy is tall and built square, solid muscle. He looks like one of those wrestlers on Latenite TNT. For the first couple of games, which we split, Mr. Gangster and Mr. Wrestler only curse at each other every couple of points or so. But as the series tightens, the insults get more personal and complex. Common nouns like "Asshole!" and "Prick!" become simple sentences like "Screw you!" and "Eat me!" Before long, mothers and sisters are performing compound complex acts of lewdness with unlikely objects,

25

multiple partners, barnyard animals. Finally, near the end the deciding game, Mr. Wrestler spikes the ball hard into Mr. Gangster's face, and Mr. Gangster charges the net.

Mr. Wrestler stops Mr. Gangster short with a punch that sounds like a car door slamming. Then, after a couple of solid body-blows, he throws Mr. Gangster to the ground and uses his face to uproot a patch of Harry's Bermuda grass. If the red light weren't on, the camcorder not rolling, I'd be cheering out loud. But just as it looks to be all over, Mr. Gangster rolls out from under Mr. Wrestler and leaps to his feet.

Brass knuckles flash in the sunlight. A looping roundhouse connects with Mr. Wrestler's head, and he goes down in a slow-motion shower of blood with Mr. Gangster on top of him, banging away. The sound of each blow is like a shovel plunged into soft ground. Drops of blood spatter the volleyball players as they stand in their places, stunned as the look on Mr. Wrestler's face when Mr. Gangster gouges out an eye.

At last, Mr. Gangster stands up. He glances down at the man on the ground like something he just scraped off his shoes. He struts over to Lethy and kisses her on the mouth. Then he pulls back and mumbles something.

There is blood on my mother's face, and she is laughing.

"Call 911!" somebody yells, as Mr. Gangster strolls off toward Eeyore's Birthday Party like nothing has happened. Then everyone takes it up. "Call 911! Call 911!"

It takes an ambulance fifteen minutes to cover the block and a half from Pease Park. Police swarm across the yard and make a commotion. But the man on the ground is dead. Mr. Gangster is long gone. Finally, a couple of blue uniforms trot back in the direction of Eeyore's while the rest run a bright yellow tape around the volleyball court. Then everybody starts asking questions.

Suddenly, Harry yells, "I've got the whole thing on tape!"

The commotion moves into the house. Harry leads some cops into the living room and sets up the VCR. The men in blue gather around the TV. Then Harry slips away into the back, where Lethy has been laying low since the first policeman walked into the yard. I hear the two of them screaming at each other even over the shovel-in-soft-ground sound of brass knuckles being rewound and rewound and rewound.

"What the hell is this?" Harry yells. There comes a wood-ripping noise, a splintering like the false back being torn out of a panty drawer. "Not only screwing some *pachuco*, but bringing this shit into our home!"

"I'm not a fucking saint like you!"

"Then be a mother."

"I am a mother!"

"No. Junkies can't be mothers. Every time you cook up this shit, you're cooking up your family."

"What do you want me to do?"

"Raise your daughter."

"Goddamn you, Harry. Don't you think I've tried? I can't stay clean."

I hear a door slam. Then another. The last glimpse I catch of my mother is a hot pink tube-top and canary yellow shorts headed toward Pease Park.

Eeyore's Birthday Party goes on until sunset. The police leave the house not long after that. They offer to station a man with us, but Harry says that we want to be alone.

We keep the doors locked tight and every light in the place blazing, each of us afraid in our own way. I am afraid that Mr. Gangster will come back and kill Harry because he told about the tape. Harry is afraid that my mother won't come back at all. He says he fears that he has laid too wide a chalk line for her to step back inside.

We watch the late local news for word of Mr. Gangster. The local CBS affiliate has a new anchor, a national-level talent; and I've been watching every night to see how she develops. She's got the right look, the great transitions, the steely-eyed stare that makes it plain only the Apocalypse will shake her. But there is something missing—that Connie Chung knack of softening her face muscles as the victims flash across the screen and fade, to let the audience know she feels their pain.

They run Mr. Wrestler's murder as the feature story. It turns out that his name was Raymond Murray and he was twenty-eight years old, an Austin native. As the anchor reads the teleprompter—her eyes almost unmoving—they flash *live footage* across the blue screen, shot hours ago, of bright yellow police tape around the blood-stained volleyball court on our front lawn. Harry's NO JUNK ALLOWED sign hangs in the background, nailed firmly to the porch. Behind the sign, Harry's rocking chair sits empty. The unknown assailant, the anchor says, remains at large.

"*Cacahuete*," Harry says, "it's going to be a long night."

"We still have practically the whole half-hour left," I say. "They may do an update, or run a late-breaker to cap off the newscast."

We sit and watch them scroll through the rest of the features, the weather, and the sports. The rain forest still on fire in Guatemala. Smoke over Texas. Sure enough, there is a late-breaking newsflash. The promising young anchor breaks into a local interest segment about speed traps with the story of another murder. Police have not yet identified the second victim, she says, but the M.O. is the same. A Hispanic female, twenty-five to thirty-five years of age, wearing a pink top and yellow shorts, found in the vicinity of Pease Park, beaten beyond recognition.

"I'll rip out his heart!" Harry yells, leaping up from his seat beside me.

The words *beyond recognition* play and replay in my head like a VCR tape that keeps rewinding. I watch the promising local anchor as she recaps the two murders, waiting to see if tonight is the night she will put it all together—to see whether or not she feels my pain. But

they fade out on file footage of those Indians in Guatemala, watching the world burn and waiting on rain.

The Comforts of Home

"*¡Abuelita!*" I hear, over the sudden pounding on my kitchen door. "*¡Abre la puerta! Tengo un regalito para ti.*"

It is the voice of my grandson, loud and demanding as it has been since Danny was a baby, left alone—first by the running-off of his teenaged mother, then by the heroin overdose of his worthless father—for me to raise.

"Speak English, Danny!" I answer, like I always do when he speaks Spanish to me. Then I get up from the table, where I have been sitting over the Tarot cards since I saw the murders on the ten o'clock news, searching for some sign that Danny is okay. But what I have seen has been of no comfort, with trouble card following trouble card—five of cups, five of wands, five of swords, five of disks: all four of the fives in a single spread.

"I have a gift for you, Granny," he says again. "Open the door."

"It's three o'clock in the morning!" I say, as I open the heavy wooden front door, then unlatch the screen door. "Where on earth have you been?"

But then I see my grandson holding the rocking chair from the 10 o'clock news—the same rocker I saw five hours ago behind a yellow crime scene tape on TV—and the answer to my question strikes me with a blow that makes my fingers shake as I reach up and re-hook the latch on the screen door.

The truth sometimes comes to me in flashes like lightning bolts from the finger of God. Other times I must read the Tarot cards, or chart planets and stars, to tease out the pattern that binds the things that have happened already to the things that have yet to come. But tonight, with the four fives of strife spread out on my table and the rocking chair from the Eyewitness News on my porch, the pattern is clear.

"Oh Danny," I say. "You hurt those people. And you stole their chair."

"Not this chair, *Abuelita*. I found it next to a dumpster over on South 2nd, and I thought of you." He sweeps an arm at the yard full of tables and chairs gleaming in the porchlight behind him—cast-offs that I have rescued and restored, sanding and staining and sealing them all by hand. "Now open up. I need a shower and some hot food. You know? The comforts of home."

"Danny," I say, looking closely at the chair, "I need you to tell me the truth. I saw this same rocking chair, with the same moon and stars carved into the headrest, sitting on the porch of the house where that man was beaten to death. *Beyond recognition*, they said. They said a woman was killed, too. The description they gave of the killer sounded just like you."

"I love you, Granny," he says. But his eyes are ugly slits. "Open the door."

It comes to me in a flash that these are the eyes of Danny's father—the same eyes Danny's father must have turned on the teenaged girl who would later give birth to my grandson. Comfortless eyes. Eyes without love. The same kind of eyes that Cain turned on Abel. The last thing those poor people on the Eyewitness News ever saw in their lives.

"You have your father's eyes," I say.

"*¡Cuidado, bruja!*" he says, pressing a hand against the screen at the spot where the latch hooks onto the doorframe. I can see, in the glare of the porch light, the ghostly remains of the blood that Danny has tried to wash off his skin.

"Speak English, Danny," I say without thinking, slitting my eyes back at him like the witch he says I am. "I see the mark of Cain on your hands."

"Don't try that *mal de ojo* bullshit on me."

There is something in Danny's voice that makes me

look away, down at the rocking chair. I can see that all the rocker needs is some sanding, two or three coats of stain, and a coat of wood sealer. With a couple of days of work, I can make it whole again. I have always had the knack of fixing broken things. But when I look back at my grandson, I don't even know where to begin.

"You've grown away from me," I say.

"Like father, like son."

"No," I say. "You have surpassed your father." I did not need to read the Tarot cards, or to chart planets and stars, to know that the two of them would come to bad ends—the father a drug addict and a statutory rapist; the son a drug addict, a cold-blooded killer, and a thief.

"What do you mean?"

"You have done him one better," I say, moving quickly away from the door. I dig out the rainy day money that I keep in a baggie in the bottom of my big flour bucket and move slowly back toward the screen, holding the clear plastic bag up so Danny can see the bills. Sixty-four dollars. It is all I have.

"What's that?" Danny asks.

"All the comfort that either one of us is going to get."

"Granny, open up. I won't take the money. And if you let me in, I won't hurt you."

"Of course you will," I say, pulling the bills from the baggie and slipping them under the screen door. "And if you don't leave now, I'll call the police."

The look in Danny's eyes, as he reaches down to take the money, would freeze the heart of a Bible hero. But I meet his gaze calmly, having nothing left to lose. He turns away, finally, picking up the rocking chair and throwing it off the porch. It hits one of the restored chairs in my yard, and I watch them tumble over each other as Danny steps away from the door.

"*Adios, bruja*," Danny says, fading from the porch light.

"Speak English, Danny," I say. "Go with God."

But I know he will go to the devil, and I will stain the rocking chair red as the mark of Cain.

Pink Dolphin

My seven-year-old son, Crockett, stands five and a half feet tall, weighs 140 pounds, and wears a man's size eight shoe. He is hardly a toddler, although most of the time he acts like one. The rest of the time, he's asleep. Crockett has autism; and so with him, anything and everything can be a major ordeal.

It was all too much of an ordeal for Crockett's father, Travis, who slipped away for the last time four years ago in the middle of a Friday night, leaving me to wake up alone on a Saturday morning in our crappy rent house in South Austin with Crockett—who had just been officially diagnosed with autism—and with a boatload of unpaid bills and the rent past-due. When Travis left, he took the rent check with him. I cried for two days. Then I got up Monday morning, and found a job and a roommate. I won't say I've never looked back. But I will say that I've never seen Travis, or the rent check, since. If I had my choice right now, I'd take the rent check.

Travis was never much good anyway, as no one with a junk habit can ever be much good. I think back on all of the broken promises and outright lies—about how he'd kick it this time, "No surrender, Annie, hold until relieved," and how he'd stick with his family this time, protect us against all comers, "Line in the sand, Annie, line in the sand." It was Travis who decided to name our son Crockett. He went on and on about how the name would be perfect, about how Crockett and Travis had been the last defenders of the Alamo. "God and Texas!" he said. "Victory or death!" He said these were the last written words of Colonel Travis.

"Victory over what?" I asked.

"Over the Mexicans," he said.

The more I've looked back at it, over the years, the more I've become convinced that if he'd been saddled with

a 140-pound autistic seven-year-old, instead of surrounded by Mexicans, Colonel Travis would've slipped
away in the middle of a Friday night himself.

Today is another Saturday morning. But I didn't
wake up alone, and I'm not crying. I haven't cried since
the Monday morning that I went out and found a roommate and a job. I've had a lot of roommates since
then—Crockett is almost as much of an ordeal for roommates as he was for his father—but I'm still working the
same job. And of course, Crockett never changes. I look at
his face, pink in the morning sun streaming in our bedroom window. For some reason—the doctors say it has
nothing to do with his autism—Crockett's skin is pink. His
hair is almost white, and his eyes are a washed-out gray
like Barton Creek after a heavy rain. I lie here for a while
in the bed we share, feeling the warmth from the window
and looking into the face of my sleeping son. For this
moment in time, except for the pink skin, everything
could be normal. My life, my son's life, everything seems
so peaceful and so quiet and so everyday, and the breath
comes slow and easy in my chest. And it comes to me that
a real victory, a victory worth winning, would be one nice,
normal day with my son. Just one.

I have the day off from Aqua Vitae Café, the restaurant where I've been waiting tables five days a week for
the past four years to pay the rent and bills for Crockett
and myself. I always work Monday through Friday so I
can have the weekends free for Crockett. We have no
scheduled activities for today, which can be a challenge.
Actually, that's not quite true, I guess. I promised Crockett that I'd take him to Zilker Park today and let him
swim in Barton Springs Pool. But yesterday I had to put
all my week's tips from Aqua Vitae into the bank to cover
the rent check I'd already written and mailed, and I didn't
even have the lousy six bucks leftover to get Crockett and
myself into the pool.

"Zilker," Crockett reminds me, as he slurps the
chocolate Malt-O-Meal from his bowl. "Zilker Park, An-

nie." Crockett always calls me by my first name. It's one of the few things in my life that makes me feel young, and I savor it as much as Crockett savors his chocolate Malt-O-Meal.

"How about we do something else today?" I ask, ignoring the slurping. Crockett's table manners are something we've been working on, but I feel too guilty this morning to scold him.

"Zilker, Annie," he says again.

Suddenly, I have an idea. There's a little park with a playground in our neighborhood, a park that also happens to be named Zilker. Not many people know this, but there are actually two Zilker Parks in Austin. There's the big one, Zilker Municipal Park, with Barton Springs Pool and the soccer fields and the Hillside Theater. And then there's Zilker Neighborhood Park—no pool, no soccer fields, and no theater, but it does have a nice playground and it's close to our house.

So I strap Crockett into the passenger seat of the battered black VW Beetle I've been driving since high school, and hand him his sippie cup, and we head over to Zilker Neighborhood Park.

"Zilker," he says as we walk away from the car. Then he gives me an accusing look. "Zilker, Annie."

"This is Zilker Park," I tell him. "Zilker Neighborhood Park."

The distinction is lost on Crockett. As we walk onto the playground, hand in hand, Crockett's head hangs like a dog's that has just been punished, and I feel the breath come sharp and shallow in my chest. There are a few other mothers and kids in the park, but the other kids avoid Crockett in exactly the same way the other mothers avoid me. So I sit alone in the shade and watch Crockett play by himself in the bright sun. While he goes back and forth between the swings and the jungle gym, I sit on a bench trying not to feel like a total failure as a human being because I don't have the money to get us into Barton Springs.

It isn't just my son's disappointment that makes me feel this way. Seeing Crockett in the water is good for me, too. Although Crockett is awkward on land, he is beautiful in the water—a natural swimmer, cutting through the water effortlessly, diving and surfacing like a dolphin at play. Crockett and I taped a program on PBS about dolphins in the Amazon River. It is a program we watch often. These river dolphins are pink—Crockett is very excited about this—and they swim beside the cargo boats, sporting in the murky water and blowing spray. Crockett looks like that when he's swimming, like a pink dolphin gliding effortlessly along, at home in his element. At play. The official name for the species is *Inia geoffrensis*. But they are *bufeo colorado* to the Peruvians who have a legend that the spirits of drowned people enter the bodies of pink dolphins; and that on moonlit nights, they change into handsome, impeccably dressed young men in white who carry off the women they seduce to an enchanted city beneath the water.

But here in Zilker Neighborhood Park, there is no moon and no river. The blinding noon sun burns down out of the breathless Texas sky. After Crockett grows tired of the swings and jungle gym, he blurts out, "Take a walk."

This is one of his few phrases that are easy to understand. I'm tired of the playground myself, so we leave the park and head slowly down Ann Arbor Lane to Rabb Glen Street. I follow Crockett as he walks and walks, wondering where he's headed. I finally realize that there are dogs barking in the distance, and Crockett is trying to find the dogs. He loves dogs almost as much as pink dolphins. So I let him trudge on. After all, I tell myself, it's a Saturday and we're in a decent neighborhood where there is almost no traffic. But then Crockett turns onto Bluebonnet Lane and starts to pick up speed toward Lamar Boulevard with all its fast-moving cars. I'm actually having to jog now, to keep up with him.

After going beyond what I think is wise, I say, "Okay, time to go back."

But Crockett keeps on moving in a kind of staggering run. If he were three years old, I could scoop him up onto my shoulders and that would be that. But he is too big to lift, let alone carry. I have no choice but to play a dirty trick.

I turn around and say, "Crockett, I am going back now. Bye-bye." There is a long, heartrending moment where I hear him pause, no longer headed for the Lamar traffic, but not headed back for the car either. Finally, I hear him start to follow. Good, no tantrums, I tell myself as I look back to check Crockett's progress. Oftentimes, when I try this trick on Crockett, he responds by throwing a fit.

We are two blocks from the car when Crockett stops suddenly and the tantrum begins. This isn't just an embarrassing inconvenience. Crockett sometimes gets so violent in his fits that he can hurt himself, or me. This one looks bad. He hops around on one foot and throws himself to the pavement, kicking and screaming the entire time. I grab him to see if he is bleeding, but he is okay this round. So far.

"Okay, baby," I say, trying to talk calmly and soothingly even though I feel like I'm about to explode. "We are almost back to the car. Let's go."

Crockett gets on all fours as if to get up and agree to walk. Then suddenly he changes his mind and starts hitting himself in the face and flopping around on the ground like a fish out of water. I'm breathing heavily now, the breath sharp again in my chest. I find myself thinking again about victory, about why we can't just have one nice, normal day when a trip to a playground can mean simply a trip to the playground—not a struggle of life or death. I'm feeling sorry for Crockett, because whatever he's going through sure isn't fun for him, and I can't do much to help. I wonder if he's hungry. I wonder if his stomach hurts. I wonder if he's feeling worn out yet, like I am.

After more of the same, we finally get back to the car and I discover a possible explanation for what's been making him so miserable. Crockett couldn't have been comfortable walking with what he was carrying in his very large diaper. Crockett still wears diapers. The doctors say that he probably always will.

I spend ten minutes taking care of business, sweat dripping down my nose, arms aching, and a headache approaching. Once Crockett is dressed and buckled in, I hand him his sippie cup, which he grabs in desperation as we pull away. We're going home. The battle is over, at least for today.

Love in Dead Languages

If you're looking for irony, Annie, you're not gonna find it here. I'm telling this straight. The last guy I told this to kind of laughed, and asked was I being ironical. So I asked him to say what type. "Comical?" he asked. Me with my heart in my hand, and him prissy, snickering in his beer. I told him I spent four years in the 82nd Airborne Division, learning ways to shove *comical*. He plunked down his beer and bailed out of the bar.

It all started with that filthy apartment. I can't stand apartments. They make me more angry than anything else I know. Sometimes just the sight of apartment walls is enough to send me into a rage. Much less being inside one, living in one. I'm talking tragic epic, Annie. Like the rage of Achilles that brought the Argives so much grief. I burned my last apartment to the ground.

It hasn't always been this way between me and apartments. The first place I ever lived, outside of the barracks and my parents' place growing up, was T.C. Jester dorm—a high-rise kind of half-assed apartment complex, about three parts teenage daycare and one part country club. This was here in Austin, at the University of Texas, in the biggest dormitory on earth. I lived on the outdoor-recreation oriented, co-ed floor. It was a thing of beauty. Every single co-ed on that outdoor-rec floor had requested it in advance. So we were all of us, from even before the outset, there for all the wrong reasons. What the hell did I care? I was twenty-two, they were eighteen, the drinking age was twenty-one. It doesn't take a sociologist to do the people math on that one. For the first time in my life, I was in demand. I was fresh out of the army, flush with college fund money, in the best drinking shape of my life, my room—seven nights a week—full of co-eds whose sole focus was swilling federally-financed beer.

Hey, while we're on the subject, who's thirsty? Hey! Down at the end there. You thirsty? Just FYI, sir, *tipping* is not a city in Taiwan. Jesus Christ! Nine out of ten people you meet in this town are skinflint alcoholics, free-loading smack addicts, or both. No offense meant, sir.

Yeah right, Annie. Maybe it's the job.

If the start of the story is that filthy apartment, then the heart of it is Ben. Ben wasn't much of a drinker. He just waddled into my dorm room one day to make friends. That was exactly how he put it. "I just waddled in to make friends." And that was how he kept on putting it, waddling in day after day and saying the same thing, "I just waddled in to make friends," looking like a cross between a teddy bear and a walrus, balding already at eighteen. He had this big round teddy bear belly and this frumpy walrus mustache that both jiggled when he said, "I just waddled in to make friends," in this deep brown teddy-walrus voice, "I just waddled in to make—"

"Friends!" I screamed one day. I cut him off. I couldn't take it even once more. "Hey, Ben! How many days does it take? How many times do I have to hear that word again?"

"Until you make . . . well, you know . . . with me," he said.

I knocked on Ben's door the next morning at dawn and asked him to breakfast. We played basketball the next afternoon, a one-on-one game in which Ben didn't make a single basket, but did manage to explain Book Four of the *Iliad* by Homer, over which I had a major test the next day. It was the craziest thing. This big teddy-walrus looking guy waddling around the court, quoting stats about Achilles and Patroclus in dead languages—it turns out that Ben's dad had taught him freaking Latin and Greek—and missing the backboard two shots out of three. Before I knew what hit me, I was spending a lot less time in my dorm room getting co-eds drunk and a lot more time making friends with Ben. He tutored me on the roots of Western culture. I coached him on the fundamentals of basketball. Over the course of our two-semester one-on-

one series, Ben got to be the best plus-sized player I've ever seen—slow to the basket, but a real master of the no-look pass, and money from outside the three-point arc—while I learned enough about ancient Greece and Rome to get me through Classic Civ. I and II.

What was that about irony, Annie?

Well, there are three types. I'll explain them to you the same way Ben explained them to me. I remember him standing there at the top of the key, dribbling thoughtfully, his red teddy bear face dripping puddles of sweat onto the white-hot concrete. "*Verbal* irony is like sarcasm," he said. Then he made a break for the basket, pulled up short, and swished a jumper while I was still back-pedaling. "Nice defense, coach." His walrus mustache gleamed in the sun when he grinned at me. "See? Verbal irony is the easiest of the three. The second type is a little tougher. With *dramatic* irony, the audience knows something a character doesn't. Pretend I'm the audience." He faked a high no-look pass and belly-laughed when I yanked my hands up to protect my face. "The audience knew I wasn't going to throw that pass. Get me?"

"I'd say you got me."

"That's the trouble with dramatic irony. You're always laughing at people, instead of laughing with them. *Cosmic* irony is even tougher. With cosmic irony, everything you do to make one thing happen leads to the opposite outcome instead."

"You mean like Fate?" I asked.

"It's more like Karma," he said. "You do something wrong and get punished. You have to be wrong-headed about something big. Your comeuppance shows both the audience, and you, the error of your ways. Like when Achilles should've been helping the Argives defend their ships, but was trying to save his reputation—and wound up losing Patroclus instead."

With a lot of help from Ben, I managed to pass enough courses so Uncle Sam didn't cut off my college fund money. Then when the year was up, we moved into that filthy apartment together with another unflunked-out guy from our floor named Pete. That apartment was such a sewer, we had to leave all the doors and windows wide open to keep from choking to death on the stink. While the rotten food fog drifted out on the cross-breeze, the rats and roaches and ants drifted in across the 70's shag. The carpet was jungle-punch-colored, a plush-piled hot pink, with black bongwater polka-dots around the couch. Dirty yellow dishes sat around in unused and out-of-the-way places—my study desk, the kitchen sink—slowly being swallowed by deep green fuzz, their contents feeding the vermin we could hear rustling among the pizza boxes in the rare moments when Pete wasn't jamming on his electric guitar or blasting a CD.

Pete had such a kicking stereo system that half the other unflunked-out folks from the outdoor-rec floor tried to bribe him into moving in with them. Ben hadn't wanted any part of the Pete auction, but I was determined to win. When Pete cranked the amps to his sub-woofer, he vibrated dorm windows three floors down. He also shot a hot game of hoops—he had a deadly baseline jumpshot, and a lightning break to the basket that you had to open up the jumper to stop—and he could do "Pretty Woman" just like Roy Orbison on his electric guitar. I got him for a lakeview master bedroom with his own private bath-room, and a fake ID with his picture and my birthday.

Does that sound ironical to you, Annie? Then name the type.

Actually, I think Ben would've agreed with me that irony usually fits pretty neatly into one of the three. But back to the sewer. There were moments of real brotherhood in that cesspool of an apartment, between Ben and Pete and me. We competed together, trying to beat out each other's brains at tackle basketball while building a sense of esprit de corps and honing our combat skills. We went to bars together and hit on party girls with body piercings and funky tattoos. That is, Pete and I did. In this New Age hippy hotbed of ecstasy and Viagra—where everybody who's anybody is out there doing something weird with somebody—Ben went to bars chemical-free and told half-naked women with raunchy studs in their tongues and rainbow snakes on their bellies that he'd just waddled in to make friends. And get this: we once played tackle basketball against the UT football team. Well, against three of them anyway—a two-eyed Cyclops and twin Ajaxes, setting blind-side picks that would've laid the ass of Achilles out flat on the hot concrete.

Yes, I mixed the *Odyssey* and the *Iliad*, Annie. Consciously.

Well, the point here isn't consistency of Homeric allusion, it's showing the bond of brotherhood between Ben and Pete and me. Like I was saying, the Cyclops set a blind-side pick on me the first time down the court. Laid me out. Slap! Face-down on that concrete pancake griddle. The second time down, I took out the bastard's hairy knees. When they pried us apart, my nose was bloody. But we'd both gotten in enough good licks so they didn't try that again on me. And Pete was so slippery and wiry that they had a hard time setting a solid pick on him. Ben, though. Ben got knocked down more times that day, harder, on that hot concrete, than anybody I've ever seen keep getting up again. He didn't just get back up, either. That was the thing. He'd hop up laughing about getting laid out, shake the hand of the blind-siding bastard who'd done it, and tell the guy, "Nice pick."

No, that wasn't verbal irony, Annie.

That was just Ben. Before long we were all laughing with him, not at him. At the end of that brutal best-of-three series—which Ben and Pete and I took from Cyclops and company two games to one—all six of us headed back to our foul-smelling cave, and while five of us swilled cheap keg beer, Ben guzzled Gatorade.

We were so close back in that filthy apartment, it was like we shared a single skin. We even managed to get along with the roaches, and to mostly ignore the ants. The ants were almost invisible in that plush-piled pink shag, and the roaches kept out of our way. The rats, though. Well, let's just say the rats didn't keep out of our way. With their talent for sneak-thieving and hiding, you'd think that rats would move through the kitchens and bedrooms of our lives like a whiff of outhouse breeze, obnoxious but unseen. But rats are vicious, and they tend to get cocky—that vicious brand of cockiness you sometimes see in mugshot smiles, bone-white teeth like a compound fracture, red beady eyes. The rats in that filthy apartment had it made. All that food laying around, all those easy pickings, a five hundred CD library, and the latest in stereo sound.

Until they attacked Ben. Ben and I shared the smaller upstairs bedroom as a result of my winning bid for Pete. And one night while I was up late getting some overdue use out of my study desk, I looked up from my *Complete Works of Aristotle* and saw a medium-sized gray rat crawling across the sleeping Ben. The rat crouched on Ben's shoulder and glared at me with red beady eyes. Then he flashed a bone-white smile, and bit a hunk out of Ben's right ear.

Let me tell you, Annie, there was nothing ironical about the screams.

"Blood! Aaahh! Hairyfangsmonsterblood!" The screams came from Ben. At least to begin with, along with a bunch of hopping around and a surprising amount of blood—it being a more than medium-sized hunk that had been bitten out of Ben's ear. In the confusion, the rat managed to sneak away and hide. Ben's screams woke up Pete, who came running in from the master bedroom and got splattered with the same bright red drops that Ben was slinging all over me.

"Blood!" Pete screamed, as red spots bloomed on his white boxers. "Stop hopping around! You're getting that shit all over me!"

"Throat!" Ben screamed, hopping and spinning and slinging blood in streaks. "Throat! Aaahh! What if he'd gone for my throat?"

Then the hopping and screaming ceased. We all stared at one another, listening hard. We all rubbed our throats. The familiar rustle of vermin among the pizza boxes was suddenly transformed into the scrape of fangs

45

and claws.

We spent the rest of the night at the emergency room, trying to come up with a rat removal plan. Anyway, Pete and I did. Ben spent most of his night applying direct pressure to what was left of his right ear. Now, rat removal might not seem like much of a problem if you've never been victimized. Hire an exterminator, you're about to say. Get a cat. But that bastard rat had done more than just bite off most of Ben's right earlobe. He'd swallowed our spirits, digested our self-confidence, crapped on the sanctity of our beds. We wanted vengeance on a personal level. We wanted to flash that bone-white smile back at him.

Anyway, Pete and I did. But vengeance on a personal level turned out to be a problem for Ben. Despite insult, injury, and a painful rabies shot, Ben refused to let Pete and me harm a single hair on that rat bastard's head. "Turn the other cheek," Ben kept saying. "Let he who is without sin cast the first stone." Maybe that came from having missionary parents—Mormons, in Sudan, I swear to God—or from studying the Bible in Latin and Greek. Ben was all the time talking about *philios*, which he said meant brotherly love. Not the kind Pete and I went looking for in bars.

I don't think it's ironical, Annie, to say that the first thing we did was clean.

We unstuck the moldy dishes from the sink bottom, piled them into cardboard boxes, and threw them away. We scraped off fungus, shoveled up pizza boxes, and shampooed the hot pink shag. Next came industrial grade poison for the roaches and ants—the bug massacre was inflicted by Pete and me, while Ben waddled out to buy rubber gloves—and so many whiteners and brighteners for the kitchen counter and sink that by the time Ben got back with the gloves, Pete and I had no skin on our hands left to save. Finally, we closed all the windows and propped open the front door, hoping that the same toxic fumes driving us out onto the back balcony would drive the rats down the front steps.

We hunkered down in our sleeping bags, there among all those other balconies with their barbecue pits and their mountain bikes and their beer kegs floating in trashcans full of melting ice, and waited for our rat infestation to drift back out the same way it had drifted in. We slept and waited, and waited and slept, looking up at all those other balconies—ours was on the second of six floors—and feeling like we were living in Hades. We took turns on watch, listening all night long, three long nights running, to the rustle of rat feet sneak-thieving and hiding, looking for any scrap of human flesh that might be left.

Then the cold front came in. It was one of those blue northers that howl down out of the Arctic and into the bone marrow of the Lone Star State, dropping temperatures into the teens and driving sleet like ice-arrows against bare skin. I knew there could be no more hunkering down in our sleeping bags. We were going to have to face the rat problem head-on. But Ben still wouldn't give in. He wouldn't let Pete and me kill the rats openly and honestly. And even worse, he wouldn't waddle out to buy more rubber gloves so we could kill them on the sly.

"Ben!" I shouted, my voice rising like a battle cry over the howling wind. "Damn it, these are rats we're talking about!"

"Rats!" Pete shouted.

"Turn the other cheek," Ben said. His voice, calm as always, carried clearly over the violence of the wind. A gentle force seemed to fill it. "Let he who is without sin cast the first stone."

"Not stones! Poison!" I shouted. "Poison, Ben! It's practically painless! Hell, it's *pink*! They just eat this pink shit and go to sleep!"

"Pink painless poison, Ben!" Pete shouted. "It sounds pretty good to me!"

"Eating that poison makes rats swell up like balloons," Ben said in that same gently powerful voice. "They vomit blood and drag themselves through it. Sometimes their bellies burst while they're still alive, and they start to chew on their own insides."

"So what?" I asked.

"So they scream. Once back in Sudan, Muslim forces shelled the Christian village my parents and I were living in. Some of the buildings caught fire. As the flames spread, burning rats started to run out of the huts. They screamed just like babies. Have you ever heard a burning baby scream?"

"So what do we do instead?" Pete asked.

"We trap them," Ben said.

"Now you're talking!" I said. "I'll go out and buy a dozen of the biggest rat traps I can—"

"No," Ben said. "Not like that. If we blow smoke into the space between the apartment walls, the rats will think the place is on fire and come running out. Once we've got them out in the open, we should be able to chase them down."

"What are we going to do with the rats, once we've caught them?" Pete asked.

"Flick them," Ben said.

"*Flick* them?" I asked. "What the hell does that mean?"

But Ben had already opened up the sliding glass door and started dragging our barbeque pit inside.

Smoke, smoke, and more smoke. That was Ben's recipe for rat removal. While he built a charcoal inferno in the barbeque pit, Pete and I tracked down every hole the rats had gnawed in the walls, and plugged all of them but two. Next Ben hauled out a black plastic tube he had gotten God knows where, and stuffed one end onto the smokestack of the barbecue. Then he threw a couple of plastic bags onto the coals and funneled the free end of the tube into one of the two remaining ratholes. Finally, we took all the yellow soup bowls that were left in the kitchen and gathered around the single rathole that was still unplugged.

It wasn't long before the smoke from the plastic bags, having filled the space between the walls, started pouring out of the hole. We stood around for a while with bowls in our hands, choking on toxic fumes. Then we heard a frantic scrabbling of claws; and about two seconds later, we saw the first rat scramble out of the wall. Rats clawed their way out one by one after that—scorched, sooty, even more smoke-addled than us—and one by one, we slapped soup bowls over their heads. We caught five of them that way, four that came out in quick succession and one that held out for what seemed like an eternity in that smoky hell. Until finally, there were five bright yellow soup bowls bottom-up on our deep-piled pink shag with textbooks on top to keep the rats from slithering out from underneath.

But we weren't finished yet. We poked around in the mattresses and box springs. We shook out the couch and chairs. Then we ran down the two rats that came scrambling out, caught them both under bowls with belly-flopping leaps, and pinned them under textbooks as well. When this second phase was over, there were seven bright yellow soup bowls bottom-up on the pink carpet, with seven textbooks perched on top—five downstairs by the barbeque pit and two upstairs next to Ben's single bed.

The time had come to flick the rats. Under Ben's direction, we slid the bowls carefully across the carpet, the rats butting their heads against the bowls and scrabbling their claws under the edges in a last-ditch attempt to escape. Then we slipped the bowls one at a time across the metal track that held the sliding glass door—a delicate maneuver that required four hands to keep the rats from squeezing through that quarter-inch of free space. Outside on the balcony, the north wind whipped sleet into our faces. Our eyelashes were so caked with ice that we had to squint to see. Smoke from the barbecue pit billowed out of the apartment and into our eyes as we lined up the downstairs rats at the edge of the balcony, five bright yellow bowls in a row underneath the black wrought-iron railing.

Like snapping off a jumpshot, the trick to rat-flicking is in the wrist. We had to snap the bottoms of the bowls just as they cleared the edge of the balcony in order to zing the rats—with a slight backspin and an arcing trajectory—across onto the grassy slope of the drainage ditch so that they rolled to the bottom unhurt, shook themselves off, and scurried away. Five snaps of five bowls. Five rats flipping backward in beautiful arcs, eyes wide open and claws clutching air—tail over face over tail over face—and we were only two bowls away from indoor sleeping, rat-free and easy, safe again in our own beds.

Ben said once that irony works best when the audience sees it coming. Tell me, Annie: What do you see?

I mean, cheap-assed apartment walls, soft plastic tubing, superheated smoke from a barbeque pit? It doesn't take a Fire Marshall to do the disaster math on that one. Less than a minute after the last of the downstairs rats had back-flipped its way through the sleet-lashed air and rolled down the grassy slope of the drainage ditch, the three of us romped in off the balcony, hooting and hollering despite the choking pall of smoke, and racing upstairs to see who would get to flick the other two. Then all at once—like some crazy reverse-miracle— the apartment walls dissolved in bright yellow flames. One minute we were triumphant, surrounded by soot-stained walls that were free of rats for the first time in months; and the next minute we were trapped like the rats them- selves, the apartment a fiery yellow soup bowl slamming down on our scorched and smoke-addled heads. The triumph on our faces faded into terror. Anyway, on Pete's and mine it did. The look on Ben's face as he bolted the rest of the way up the stairs was one I'd never seen in my life.

"Ben!" I yelled.

"No!" Pete yelled.

The apartment walls roared hellfire. Then the stairs started to crumble, and Pete and I threw ourselves out onto the balcony, scaled the wrought iron rail, and leapt for our lives—spinning slowly around to strike the slope of the drainage ditch, roll over and over in the wet grass, and look back for some sign of Ben. But our apartment

50

had turned into flame.

We sat in the driving sleet and watched the whole apartment building burn. The north wind sometimes whipped the flames a hundred feet up into the air, sometimes lashed them down into the building again. Bright red pumpertrucks arrived, sirens singing. A bunch of burly guys in yellow raincoats herded other bleary-eyed residents into the drainage ditch, while more yellow-raincoated guys stood around with firehoses and wet the rest of the complex down.

Hard on the heels of the fire department came the police. They said it was a miracle that more than one person hadn't died. If the neighbors hadn't been away, or if Pete and I hadn't been quicker, the body count would have climbed. Pete and I had been lucky, they said.

When I asked if they were being ironical, they said it never crossed their minds.

The apartment managers, who came hard on the heels of the police, never once used the word *lucky*. "Criminal negligence," they said. "Willful destruction of property," they said. Those same words were taken up by the police just before they took out their handcuffs. And then rights were read. Charges and countercharges flung back and forth. Lawsuits filed.

We blamed it all on Ben. We told the police and the apartment managers that the whole thing was Ben's idea, and that we'd tried to stop him. "Ben lost his mind," we said. "He spent all his time waddling around on the basketball court, talking about love in dead languages and the sound of babies burning alive."

What else could we do? His missionary parents didn't have any property for the apartment complex lawyers to take. They'd already lost everything that they had to lose. A long time before the last of it was over, on a lead-gray day in Austin, Texas, they loaded up what was left of Ben and flew it to Salt Lake City—home of Ben's favorite basketball team.

Go ahead. Call that ironical. But you have to name the type. Get it right, and you drink on the house all night.

Get it wrong, and—wild as I am about you, Annie—you'll have to plunk down that beer and bail out of the bar.

Prodigal of Water

I am the Prophet Mudcat. I am the one who waits for you. It is time to come home.

I sing my siren songs to you from across a great distance, but it need not always be so. You are deaf and dumb and blind in ways you cannot conceive. I will show you dimensions beyond the physical that cannot be accessed from the air.

Let this be my gift to you.

Light takes on a quality when it enters the water for which no human tongue retains a term. *Refracted? Slowed?* These words are like cinder cones on a submarine volcano whose white heat is made palpable in a spectrum that you have lost the means to perceive.

Let me show you the way.

I will give you bright blue catfish whiskers and butter-colored eyes. I will set your sensual dark ablaze with voluptuous light. Let me stretch my delicately-webbed fingers around your hips. You place yours on mine. Let us waltz together underwater among the shadowy undulations of the Milky Way.

You are not a prisoner of air, but a prodigal of water.

Let me show you the way home. Your course will be as stately as the mighty Amazon. Not at all like my own.

I had to swim for my life.

I was wending my way beneath the surface of Town Lake toward my nightly shift at the water treatment plant, a vial of newly-gleaned trendone stuck down into my Speedo and a dry-bag full of work clothes tied around my waist. The sun was setting. A heavenly explosion of orange and red light filled the water; and with every breath that flowed across my gills, I felt those glorious colors filter their way into me. I knew no passage of time, no pull of gravity. I felt completely transfigured—a powerful space-swimmer with his senses extended beyond the limits of humankind.

I said: I am the Prophet Mudcat! I have been re-made. Heated white-hot, poured into a new mold, and tempered in the waters of Town Lake. I am a fine-honed half-catfish on a holy crusade to bring love to the human race!

The salamanders said: Not a single syllable of that pompous pronouncement is literally true.

I said: But you called me a half-catfish.

They said: Those words were your own.

I said: But what about the vision? The hearing? The gills? What about the love-in?

They said: Yes, yes, yes. You have been granted all that. But those are secondary systems, mere peripherals and plug-ins. Your primary upgrade is more radical by far. You are Planet Earth's first biocomputer, equipped with a state-of-the-art parallel bioprocessor and a terabyte of RAM.

I said: Frosty as the ass end of an asteroid.

They said: At apogee. You see, the vast majority of computers on Planet Earth are as crude as their engineers. They perform operations sequentially, evaluating each possible answer separately and solving the formula over and over until a solution is finally found. But your parallel bioprocessor—your genetically modified brain—works out every possibility simultaneously, leaving your silicon-based counterparts eating cosmic dust.

I said: I understand all that. I'm a computer pro-grammer, remember? I write code.

They said: You wrote code. Now you are code.

I said: How can that be?

They said: In the entire galactic genome, there are only four types of nucleotides—A, T, C, and G—and they always form the same pairs. But the number of ways in which they can align to make up DNA strands is as myriad as the lifeforms of the Milky Way. The A-T and C-G pairs in your upgraded chromosomes are like the zeros and ones in a binary code . . .

I said: My God. I'm exponential. I'm . . . I'm . . . Wait a minute. Am I God?

The salamanders said: There is no Goddess but Love, and Mudcat is Her Prophet.

I said: Even better. I'm a lightspeed-fast hybrid disciple of Love. Let the love-in begin!

They said: If you continue to refer to yourself as a hybrid, your career as the Prophet Mudcat will be cut short.

I said: Is that some kind of threat?

They said: Have you forgotten the hospital already? Access your database. These primitive post-primates are the most aggressive xenophobes in the Spiral Arm. You must be cautious.

I said: You sound like my mother.

They said: Your mother led the—

I said: SHH!!! What's that?

At the nether edge of my much-improved hearing range, something weird had started up. A kind of high-pitched wail. It was muffled, but modulating fast—like a recorded police siren played back on fast-forward in a room full of shaving cream.

I said: What the hell is that?

The salamanders said: The Air Force assassins have launched a hovercraft downlake. We suggest immediate uplake flight!

I said: Look, I'm down here in my element, and they're stuck in thin air. How can they possibly do me any harm?

The salamanders said: With a fishfinder and dynamite.

The first charge lit up Town Lake like a supernova. I felt the shock wave roll across my body, and was inspired to put on a burst of real speed. I zoomed across the bottom, churning up silt and plastic six-pack holders in clouds as I zigzagged among brushpiles and bulls-eyed old tires. But the explosions homed in on me, each blast like an electric baseball bat swatting the hanging curve of my spine.

I said: I can't feel my legs anymore!

The salamanders said: Initiating regeneration.

Leave the water now, before it is too late!

I dragged myself up onto the jogging trail just west of the Lamar Boulevard Bridge, and clawed my way into the underbrush like a piece of roadkill. The taste of thin air in my lungs, after thick rich water, was like sucking the tailpipe on a city bus. I lay still for a long moment and listened to the breath rattle in my chest before I parted the leaves and looked back.

I said: It's too late.

The hovercraft perched on the lake like a space-age water spider, squirting fire into its prey. Banks of lights across the U-shaped prow glared like rows of compound eyes. It was floating straight for the spot where I'd crawled up on shore, stabbing searchlights out ahead of itself and leaving a trail of stunned fish and smoke and spray.

The salamanders said: Move! Move!

I said: Can you fix my legs?

I lay among the dark leaves, dead below the waist, as searchlights attached themselves to the bank around my position like filaments of web. I felt a white-hot filament attach itself to me. Then I went blind and the only thing in my head was white noise.

An assassin with a bullhorn said: ON YOUR FEET, MUTANT!

I said: Don't shoot! I've been injured!

The salamanders said: If you don't stop whining and start crawling, right now, you'll be dead!

I dragged myself out of the searchlight, arm-over-armed my way to the top of the bank, and flopped onto the grass. Half-blinded, half-crazed—but feeling the life start to burn its way back into my thighs, at least—I hauled myself up onto my still-dead feet. Then I staggered out into the open park. Hollow-point slugs and flares whizzed and popped around me like bottle rockets, and I felt a fiery wave of pinpricks washing back and forth between my spine and my knees.

I stumbled across Lamar onto the pitch-and-putt golf course, and I heard the gunshots stop. The fire in my spine had spread down through my ankles now, and I could feel my feet. Even the agony of webbed toes on wire, as I scaled the chain-link fence at the back of the pitch-and-putt course, came like a breath of cool relief.

I headed south, straight away from the lake, until I got to Barton Springs Road. Then I hooked a left onto Barton Springs and doubled back to Auditorium Shores. I was running well now—better than I could remember ever running before—feeling strong of leg and steady of stride. My breath came slow and easy, and my balance was back. As I climbed up onto the First Street Bridge, I took the concrete steps two at a time.

I said: Salamanders! How did you do that?

The salamanders said: How did we do what?

I said: Are you kidding? Ten minutes ago, I was paralyzed from the waist down. Now I'm running like a professional marathoner. How can that be?

They said: We have the ability to convert certain of your cells to other uses; and of course, to repair and redirect your neural network all the way from your brain to the tiniest nerves that permeate your body. However, our abilities are limited. In this case, fortunately for yourself and the future of your species, the damage was fairly minor.

I said: So what you're saying is that if I'd been hit in the head or the heart by one of those hollow-point slugs, or if the damage to my spine had been worse . . .

They said: Then you would be dead now, and on your way to being dissected. And there would be nothing we could do to change that.

Sobered, I stood on the walkway and looked back the way I had come, trying to figure out what to do next. Police lights flashed blue-and-white on the south bank of Town Lake now, up around the Lamar Boulevard Bridge. I saw flashlights flicker like fireflies among the trees, fanning out in a slow half-circle through the park. It was just at that moment—as I was grasping the incredibly limited nature of my life-sustaining resources, and the vast reserves of those who were trying to make me dead—that I realized I had lost my bag of clothes.

I said: Any chance of returning to the water?

The salamanders said: Not unless a pre-dawn meeting with Air Force assassins is an option you would care to explore. Why?

I said: Because we've got about three minutes before the police get here, and I seem to have lost my clothes. Any suggestions?

They said: At the risk of employing an off-color colloquialism, we suggest that you move your ass.

I climbed down off the walkway in my Speedo, crossed underneath the First Street Bridge, and cut across the grounds of the Hyatt Hotel. When I hit Congress Avenue, I headed back south in that same ground-eating stride. Finally, I slowed to my best imitation of a casual stroll and locked my eyes on the neon-lit limestone facades that stretched away up the hill.

I said: How's that for moving my ass, you insensitive piles of salamander shit?

The salamanders said: Not bad for an upgraded aborigine. Your double-looping maneuver seems to have thrown the assassins off track. They will return with a helicopter and an infrared scanner. How do you feel?

I said: You cold-blooded bastards should've asked that when I was paralyzed.

They said: Your interminable whining made it quite clear how you felt then. Now take a brief moment, assess your current condition, and make a report.

I took a long moment. I took another long moment.

I said: Let me know if I leave anything out. I've been hit by lightning, hybridized by alien social workers, sent on a love mission whose failure means annihilation or enslavement for the human race. I've been shot at, blown up, paralyzed below the waist, and now I'm the target of an all-out manhunt—make that mutanthunt—by Air Force assassins with reverse-engineered UFO technology who've hooked up with the Austin Police.

The salamanders said: We'd call that a fair assessment.

I said: Then my report is that, despite everything,

I feel better right now than I've ever felt in my life.

It was true. Through the lens of my newly-expanded senses, the most ordinary things seemed shimmering and rare, and pregnant with a significance that I had never appreciated before. The limestone blocks in the old buildings on Congress looked to my new eyes like postcards from Earth's distant past. The red neon cock-and-balls sign out in front of the Austin Motel was an alien blueprint for the shape of things to come. The message on the signboard—SO CLOSE YET SO FAR OUT—was the leitmotif of a trendone-based love opera starring yours truly, and soon to be on the lips of all humankind.

The salamanders said: Perhaps there may be hope after all, for these bare-skinned baboons.

I said: Hope, hell. You ain't heard nothin' yet.

So I sing you this siren song, my soon-to-be brothers and sisters, as I work my way back toward the water of life. The forces arrayed against us are strong and determined. But the power of love will triumph over the lies of those who seek to use fear to keep us apart.

I go before you to prepare a place where *truth* and *love* and *life* all share a single meaning. If you have courage to listen and ears to hear, you need only take heart.

I sing my siren songs to guide you home.

Words to Live By

1. *Big Picture*

5:39 a.m. Self, thirty years old. Joseph Jasmine, Ph.D. Hunched bleary-eyed over the steering wheel on my way to sling lobster and eggs, I am trying to keep my mind on the big picture.

Wife, twenty-seven years old. Son, six months. Both mine. Elizabeth and Jacob. Spooned together in the bed I've just left, they are probably asleep again after my frenzied departure from home.

Home, three bedrooms, one bath. The bank's. 3616 South 2nd Street. Built in 1983, monthly payment more than half my take-home pay from job #1, a 112 thousand dollar note at 7 ¼ percent, cosigned by my father.

Father, fifty-nine years old. Mother, fifty-six. Both mine and mine alone. Joe and Edna. They are probably sitting elbows-down at the kitchen table in the house where I grew up, finishing their second cups of coffee. They are waiting for enough daylight so the old man can check the cattle—which he believes to be the most loyal creatures on earth—and almost certainly questioning the wisdom of cosigning the oversized mortgage of their overeducated and underpaid son.

Job #1. Mine. Full-time faculty at River City Community College, a 5/5 load at $32,532 plus a coffee cup, a living wage only when supplemented by job #2.

Job #2. Mine also. Part-time waitperson at Aqua Vitae Café, $2.01 per hour plus tips, sufficient to cover my student loan payment and a mostly beans and rice diet for Elizabeth and myself. Jacob, nursing still, has no idea.

2. *Day-to-Day*

5:40 a.m. As I blow through the red light at Oltorf and South First, narrowly missing a jogger who flips me the finger, I find myself suddenly focused, white-knuckled, on the day-to-day. I pry a hand off the steering wheel, flip open my cell phone, and—remembering the recurring dream in which I am a lobster about to be tossed into a pot of boiling water—call in late to work for the second time this morning. When the phone at Aqua Vitae starts to ring, I whisper a fervent prayer: "Please God not Manager Joe, please God—"

"Aqua Vitae Café!" someone shouts into my ear. "Home of the twenty-four hour pterodactyl. Glow-in-the-dark latenite land. Birthplace of the Mother's Day Lobster Brunch. This is Bruno! How may I help you?"

"Bruno, it's Joe again," I say, feeling relief wash over me. "I'm running—"

"You mean Joe Teacher Joe, or Joe the Lead Singer of the Pixels Joe? You don't sound much like Joe Manager Joe, and anyway—"

"It's Joe Teacher Joe!" I say. "Bruno, wait!"

"—Joe Manager Joe's right here! Hold on, Joe Teacher Joe."

"No, Bruno!"

"I told you to be here by half past five," Manager Joe snarls into my ear. "That deadline passed ten minutes ago. Be here by quarter to six, or don't come at all."

"I'll be there, I swear! Just don't fire me when I walk in the door. And don't hang up! Put Bruno back on."

"Hey, Joe Teacher Joe."

"Hey, Bruno. Listen. I'll pay you ten bucks to start my brunch set-up for me. Ten bucks, Bruno, to cut and stock desserts. What do you say?"

"Sold, Joe Teacher Joe! What do I do?"

"For starters, give the phone back to Manager Joe."

"The next words out of your mouth better be: *I'm pulling into the alley right now.*"

"Even better. Bruno's agreed to start my set-up for me. If you'll just walk him through cutting and stocking desserts, and agree not to fire me, I'll work this shift off the clock."

"Slave labor, huh? Hmm . . . Words to live by. You've got serious time-management issues, Teacher Joe. But I like the way you talk."

I hang a right on Johanna, hearing the tires squeal as I fishtail once and line out. Then I whip into the alley behind Aqua Vitae Café, skid to a stop inches from the back fence, and—apron in one hand and briefcase in the other—hurdle the back gate, one-hop the patio steps, and duck in the side door.

3. *Food Mud, Keening Scream, Latenite, Aqua Vitae Café*

5:42 a.m. The only thing I can smell is the dishroom—two sinks full of food-caked pots and pans behind a partition of shelves stacked with bustubs that have been full of the ashtray-and-egg remains of too many breakfasts for too many hours. The music—some kind of weird keening scream—invades my ears in the same way the dishroom invades my nostrils. I stride up the narrow throughway that runs the length of the back of the house at Aqua Vitae Café, past the kitchen on my right and on my left coffeemakers and coffee cups and tea urns on stainless steel counters that should all be sparkling clean in the bright shift-change light but are instead dull with food mud.

The food stink and the keening scream prod my sleep-starved brain like dirty fingers as I try to tally up shift-change duties that the latenite waitpeople have left undone. Farther up on the right, I see Manager Joe's waist-length black braid whipping back and forth as he harries the much larger Bruno like a cow dog driving a herd bull. "More cutting, Bruno! Less grazing!" I hear Manager Joe bark. "The next bite of apple torte comes out of your check."

"I'm unofficially here!" I shout at Manager Joe, once I'm past his line of sight.

"Congratulations. Finish shift change by six, or— off the clock or not—it's officially your ass!"

5:43 a.m. Considering the circumstances, it could be worse. The breakfast counter is empty except for two latenite waitpeople, Gothic in black leather and multiple studs pierced through various body parts. The waitgoths—a guy with blonde dreadlocks and a junk habit named Jeremy and a girl named Chay with blue Chinese characters tattooed on her face and arms—are doing their checkouts and smoking hand-rolled cigarettes. Out on the waitfloor, beneath the trademark Aqua Vitae Café pterodactyl dangling from the ceiling on invisible wires, all four seated tables have their orders already. If I can get the Quote of the Day done, get creamers out on the tables, get coffee and tea brewed in seventeen minutes, and get the waitgoths to knock out the rest of their closing duties while I'm getting it done, I'll get to keep job #2 another day.

Through the window in the wall above the breakfast bar, I see Manager Joe still giving Bruno hell. But the keening scream is so loud I can hardly hear him. "Those back counters are still filthy," I shout in Chay's direction as I step up to the bar. "Whose closing sidework would that be?"

"Actually, that would be opening sidework," Chay shouts back at me and half-grins. Then she stabs a half-smoked butt in my direction. "Yours, for coming in fifty-eight minutes late."

"No way."

"Way!" Manager Joe snarls through the breakfast bar window, his hearing apparently more acute than mine. "Wipe down the back counters, Teacher Joe. And get it done by 6 a.m., or get the hell out!"

Chay's half-grin widens so that it wrinkles the Chinese characters on her face.

I stow my briefcase in the hoststand cabinet, pull out the magic marker bag, haul down the special board for the Quote of the Day, then squeeze into the narrow wedge of breakfast counter not already occupied by latenite waitgoths, their piles of tickets, their stacks of crumpled money, and the ash-coated remains of their breakfast food. I pull a red magic marker from the bag, grip it tightly, and—visualizing the business end as a tongue depressor mashing down on Manager Joe's offending member—I write across the top of the special board: QUOTE OF THE DAY. I pull out a green marker, and—visualizing the business end as an otoscope poking through Manager Joe's overly acute eardrums—I write across the bottom of the special board: WIN A TWO-EGG BREAKFAST! Then I pull out a black marker, stare into the vast expanse of blank white space between the red and green letters, and grope for a Latin phrase that captures my feelings about Manager Joe but does not contain the word *colonoscopy.*

I think you should write: *Accept humiliation as a surprise,*" Chay says, flicking ash onto the special board. This phrase from the *Tao Te Ching* is the quote Chay has tattooed in blue Chinese characters across her forehead. The quotes on her arms are from the *Art of War.* "Words to live by. Wouldn't you say so, Teacher Joe?"

"I think you should write something for Mother's Day," Jeremy says.

"Mother's Day and humiliation go together like lobster and eggs," Chay says. "Just ask Teacher Joe." She jabs her cigarette into my face like a smoking gun. "Besides, Teacher Joe owes me one. I'd be home by now, if I hadn't picked up those four tables for his tardy ass. And he'd be fired."

"You're right, Chay," I say. "I do owe you. And this particular Mother's Day has already been humiliating enough to surprise even me."

Manager Joe's snarling face reappears in the breakfast bar window. "I'm headed back to check the lobster tank," he says. "If you want to avoid any more surprises, you'd best get your ass in gear."

I look at Manager Joe's black braid swinging from side to side as he stalks off into the back of the house. I look down at the blank white space on the special board. Then I write, in letters the color of Manager Joe's hair: *VESCERE BRACIS MEIS.*

4. *Eat My Shorts*

5:46 a.m. "That doesn't look like *Accept humiliation as a surprise* to me," I hear Chay say over my shoulder. "What does it mean?"

"Eat my shorts."

"Eat mine, you ungrateful son of a bitch."

"No, Chay. That's what the sign says. *Vescere bracis meis.* Eat my shorts."

"Bullshit."

"I swear to God."

"Don't swear to God," Jeremy says. "It's bad karma."

"Maybe that Latin crap is good for something after all," Chay says. "*Vescere bracis meis*, Jeremy."

"*Vescere bracis meis* yourself, Chay."

"Darling!" Chay says. "Your place or mine?" She locks her mouth onto Jeremy's and blows smoke out through his nose.

5:47 a.m. I hang the Quote of the Day sign over the hoststand; I dump, clean, and rinse the coffee pots and tea urns; I put fresh coffee and tea on to brew.

5:53 a.m. I fill the creamers from the milk cow—a stainless steel milk dispenser with a valve-stem for a teat—and place fresh creamer set-ups onto all twenty-four tables on the waitfloor. Then I make a rapid-fire round beneath the dangling pterodactyl, pulling old creamers and dirty ashtrays off into a bustub and wiping all twenty unseated tables with a rag soaked in bleachwater strong enough to sterilize the floor of a barn.

5:58 a.m. I wipe the food mud off the back counters with a rag soaked in that same bleachwater, then toss the rag into a slime-filmed bleachwater bucket for the second brunch waitperson to dump.

"Time!" I yell down the throughway in Manager Joe's direction.

6:00 a.m. The weird keening scream is suddenly cut off. Everyone in the restaurant pauses. Blinks. Looks around. Then the moment of silence that marks the official transition from latenite to brunch gives way to *The Emperor Concerto*'s opening chord, and we all start moving again in E-flat major.

"Shift change!" I say, clearing the ash-coated breakfast remains from in front of Chay and Jeremy, who are still locked tight at the lips. "No more smoking. And take the lip-lock outside."

I find Bruno in the dishroom, working hard to catch up. "Hey, Joe Teacher Joe!" he says, without looking up from the twin pot-and-pan-filled sinks he would've emptied already with his bulging, tattoo-covered arms, if doing my desserts hadn't put him behind. "What's the Quote of the Day?"

"*Vescere bracis meis.*"

"Cool! What does it mean?"

"Thank you very much," I say, "in Latin." Then I step into the dishroom and slip a ten-dollar bill into his apron pocket.

"Way cool! *Vescere bracis meis*, Joe Teacher Joe!"

"*Vescere bracis meis*, Bruno," I say. "Don't forget to thank Manager Joe when he cuts you loose."

I carry the clean pots and pans back to the prep-room, thinking of Chay's sly half-grin. It's a stupid expression—about on a level with cows chewing their cuds—and probably the most obnoxious form a smile can take. But at least she was smiling. I stand in the preproom for a long moment, trying to remember the last time I smiled.

Then I catch sight of the lobster tank. There are at least two dozen lobsters, some hunched around the aerator with their claws wired closed, others crawling all over each other in a blood-colored pile. Instead of a smile, I find myself remembering my recurring lobster nightmare—and the pots and pans in my hands feel suddenly like cold metal claws as I fight for room to breathe.

It's all I can do not to duck back out the side door and run for my life.

5. *Room to Breathe*

6:02 a.m. Wife, red-haired, pale-skinned, lovely. Hopeful in the face of our house-poverty, she is probably still sleeping peacefully as the first rays of sun steal through the blinds. Her middle name is Faith, but ought to be *foolhardy*. Son, pale-skinned like his mother, all his other features mine. His middle name is Joseph, after his grandfather and me, but ought to be *Mastercard*.

Father, leather-skinned from a life spent working in the Southwest Texas sun, none of his features mine except his disposition. Stubbornly optimistic beneath a camouflage of pessimism, he is probably killing the engine of his battered work truck and starting to pair up cows and calves, listening to the rustle of the cattle—which I believe to be the stupidest animals on earth—grazing in the thick Bermuda grass, and chewing their cuds.

6. *Lobster Pot*

6:03 a.m. Self, bleary-headed in a string-tied apron and strapped-on smile. Hating Aqua Vitae, but glad not to be staring at cows engaged in nature's most brainless activity—or arguing for the hundredth time with my father about whether cattle are the most loyal, or the stupidest, animals on earth—I nod at Barkeep as he makes his regular Sunday morning entrance in a sweat-soaked workout suit, military haircut, and stubbly beard.

Barkeep nods back at me. Then he glances up at the Quote of the Day and smiles his tight-lipped ex-Airborne smile. "Eat your own shorts, buddy," he says.

Barkeep, who spent his formative years in the Airborne Infantry and now tends bar at a place up Congress Avenue, has been dating one of the Aqua Vitae waitpeople–a lifer named Annie who has an autistic child. Where Barkeep learned his Latin, I have no clue.

"Not for a million dollars, Barkeep. I know where they've been." I meet him at the breakfast bar with a cup of Aqua Vitae Blend, a fresh creamer, and a glass of water with no ice. Rather than facing the Beethoven concerto, Chay and Jeremy have retreated to the patio; and I wipe down the counter while Barkeep settles onto his usual stool. "How would you like your free eggs?"

"Scrambled this morning," he says, "with a short stack of gingerbread-blueberry pancakes on the side."

"I'll have to charge you a dollar for the blue-berries."

"*Alea iacta est,*" he says.

"Hail Caesar," I say. "I'll hang your ticket while you march on Rome."

6:05 a.m. I hang Barkeep's ticket, but there is no one in the kitchen. So I walk around to the flattop and throw the cakes down myself. I dimple the sizzling gingerbread batter with a handful of fresh blueberries, then head back around to the breakfast bar to refill Barkeep's cup. Barkeep drinks coffee faster and hotter than anyone I've ever seen.

While I splash hot, fresh Aqua Vitae Blend into Barkeep's cup, I make a visual inspection of the wait-floor. The purple Aqua Vitae pterodactyl, seen from this angle, seems to be swooping over Barkeep's shoulder. It's like a glimpse back through time into a prehistoric age—an age when work was done for the simple purpose of survival; and there were no mortgages, no student loan debts, no tables to wait, and no briefcases full of ungraded exams.

6:08 a.m. There is still no one in the kitchen. So I walk around and flip Barkeep's gingerbread-blueberry shortstack myself, then head down the line to start work on his eggs. When I look up, I see Himmler—Bruno the dishwasher's brother; the six-foot-six, shave-headed cook and Aryan Nations member who should've been here at 6 a.m.—hulking beside me, looking down.

"Hey, Teacher Joe. Thanks for getting things started. My brother says you tipped him ten dollars," Himmler says. "When the Aryan Nations avenge Waco, you will be spared. Now get your ass out of my kitchen and don't bring it back in."

"Hey, Himmler. Could you make sure the cakes and eggs on this first ticket come out hot and fresh, and together? I think my timing was a little off."

"Could you get your ass out of my kitchen? Get me some coffee while you're at it. I had a rough night."

"Thanks, Himmler," I say. "Coffee's on the way."

I set a cup of Aqua Vitae Blend on the counter at the very edge of Himmler's kitchen sanctuary, then make a refilling run—coffee pot in one hand and water pitcher in the other—by Barkeep at the breakfast bar and by all four tables of latenite leftovers still lingering on the waitfloor. By the time I'm back, Himmler is putting plates of cakes and eggs in the pickup window.

I set gingerbread-blueberry pancakes and scrambled eggs and syrup down in front of Barkeep, then slip over to the hoststand, haul a stack of final exams out of my briefcase, head back over to the counter, and—River City Community College coffee cup in one hand and red pen in the other—start making red marks on tests just as fast as my fingers will move.

"Who are today's victims?" Barkeep asks.

"Classic Civ 1613," I say. "About the only thing they remember about Rome is that it had the first shopping mall."

"Trajan's Market," Barkeep says. "AD 112."

"A-plus," I say. "I'd give you a free two-egg breakfast, but you're already eating one. How is everything?"

"It's been better, Joe. Everything has been a whole lot better."

"Don't blame me!" Himmler shouts through the window. "Teacher Joe waited too long to start the eggs."

"I'm sorry, Barkeep," I say, noticing only now that Barkeep—who usually goes through breakfast food as fast as he does Aqua Vitae Blend—has hardly touched his cakes and eggs. "It's my fault. I can't seem to get caught up these days."

"It's not the food, buddy. It's Annie. We've been seeing a lot of each other lately. Truth be told, I'd like to ask her to move in with me. But she's having major problems with her son, Crockett, and I don't want her to think I'm asking her to move in just to help her out. She's independent, you know? If I ask her to move in, I'm a male chauvinist bastard. If I don't ask her to move in, I'm a commitment-phobic son of a bitch. I feel like there's no way to win."

I look hard into Barkeep's eyes that I notice only now are bloodshot and baggy. I grope for words of encouragement, but nothing comes. "I'm sorry," I say at last.

"So am I. But I still don't know what to say to Annie. I keep trying to think of the right thing, you know? *Cogito, ergo sum*." Then he translates for Himmler, who is leaning through the window and hanging on every word: "I think, therefore I am."

"*Cogito, ergo doleo*," I say. "I think, therefore I am depressed."

"*Cogito sumere potum alterum!*" Barkeep says, and smiles his tight-lipped smile. "I think I'll have another drink!"

"I could use a drink myself," I say. "I think we all could. How about a whiskey for me, and a beer for my horse?"

"Eat my shorts, buddy. I'm off the clock. And anyway," he says, nodding in the direction of Himmler, "your horse looks like he had one too many last night. But seriously, while we're on the subject of the clock, isn't Annie here yet?"

"Not yet," I say. "She must be running late. Like the rest of us." Then, suddenly remembering that I've got papers to grade, I slap a C-minus on another test.

"Say Joe, you don't look so good yourself," Barkeep says. "What's the buzz, buddy?"

"I had a very bad dream that came true," I say.

"You and Martin Luther King!" Himmler shouts through the pick-up window.

"What was the dream?" Barkeep asks, ignoring Himmler.

"I was a lobster, with my claws wired closed. And I got tossed into a lobster pot."

"You really could use a drink, buddy," Barkeep says. "Come down to Ego's sometime when I'm working, and have a couple of drafts on the house."

"Seriously?" I ask.

"Seriously, buddy."

"I still have to charge you a dollar for those blueberries," I say.

"That's okay, buddy. The draft beer's still free."

6:28 a.m. I put the stack of graded exams into alphabetical order, place them back into my briefcase with the four stacks of finals that remain ungraded, and clear Barkeep's half-empty plates from the breakfast bar.

"Can I wrap this to go for you, Barkeep?"

"I think I'll sit here a while and wait on Annie," he says, sliding a five-dollar bill across the counter. "Keep the change. What was the final tally on those exams?"

"One A, two B's, ten C's, fourteen D's, and five F's."

"*Nil desperandum*," Barkeep says.

"Never despair?" I ask slowly. "Words to live by. If I ever get home today, maybe I'll share them with my wife."

7. *Kill, Kill, Kill Them All*

6:33 a.m. I wipe down the counter in front of Barkeep, bus the four dirty tables that the latenite leftovers have abandoned in their flight from the coming sun, then set out a two-pound bag of freshly-ground Aqua Vitae Blend beans for Harry the Hippy. Harry is another of my regulars. He comes in every Sunday morning, precisely at seven, to pick up his weekly coffee supply.

"Hey, buddy," Barkeep says, "how about a splash of that Aqua Vitae Blend for me?"

I refill Barkeep's coffee cup, then haul another stack of ungraded exams out of my briefcase. The first test I grade is a borderline D-minus/F from a student I've had problems with the whole semester—he's gone to the head of the Humanities Department twice on my account, once to complain about my ridiculous attendance policy and once to complain about my unfair grading standards—and after struggling with myself for a full two minutes, and then guiltily assigning the test a grade of C in hopes of avoiding an appeal and another trip to the head of the Humanities Department's office, it is all I can do to pick up the next exam.

"Wanna talk about it?" Barkeep asks.

"I'm in debt up to my eyeballs, I hate both my jobs, I never get to see my family, my sex life has stopped, I haven't gotten a good night's sleep since my son was born, and I started my morning by getting up late and stepping in cat shit."

"It could be worse. Anything else?"

"Yeah," I say, looking out the front window and feeling my heart sink into my filth-encrusted shoes. "A student with whom I've been having problems the whole semester, and to whom I just gave a C instead of an F on a Final Exam to keep from ever having to see him again, is about to walk in the front door with what looks like his whole family."

"Okay, it's worse. Good luck, buddy."

6:42 a.m. I lean through the pickup window and tell Himmler that we're getting a ten-top. His response would put a saint into Purgatory. Thinking of penance, I watch the family of my problem student dragging tables together on the waitfloor while I count out ten menus and silverware setups. By the time I've got everything together, they're all seated at a makeshift ten-top that takes up space enough to seat twenty. My problem student sits enthroned at the head of the table. Once I've handed out menus and silverware, I talk to him first.

"Good morning, Mr. Wiles," I say.

"Good morning, Dr. Jasmine. Nice apron."

"Thanks. Can I start you out with some coffee?"

"First let me introduce you to my mother," he says, smiling at the handsome older woman in a black formal dress who is sitting next to him. She has diamonds in her ears the size of blueberries. "Mother? Meet Dr. Jasmine. He's the teacher I've told you so much about."

"You should be ashamed of yourself," the old woman says, her eyes blazing like her diamonds.

"My father would say the same thing, ma'am, if he could see me right now. Would you like to start with some coffee?"

"Bring all of us coffee," she says. "Except the children, of course. Bring them orange juice. You do have orange juice, don't you?"

"Yes, ma'am."

"Then hop to it."

6:45 a.m. I load eight cups of Aqua Vitae Blend, two O.J.'s, and ten icewaters onto an oval tray and set them down on the Wiles's table, starting with the mother and working my way around to finish up with her son. "Are you ready to order breakfast?"

"We'll all have the lobster and eggs special," the mother says. "With buttermilk pancakes as our side orders."

"I'm sorry, ma'am," I say. "But we don't start serving lobster until 9 a.m."

"Ridiculous," the old woman says.

"But true," I say.

"We'll see about that. Bring me a manager."

6:50 a.m. Manager Joe swings open the office door after at least thirty seconds of pounding. "This had better be good," he snarls.

"The host and the second brunch waitperson are late," I say, "and there's a ten-top on the waitfloor. They all want to order lobster."

The look on Manager Joe's face is grim. "The host was supposed to be Kurt. But Kurt's having girlfriend problems, and won't be here for another hour."

"So what else is new?"

"One thing that's new, Teacher Joe, is that Kurt will be written up when he comes in. This will be his final warning. Another new thing is that the second waitperson was supposed to be Annie, who was supposed to be getting a ride to work from Kurt because that piece of shit Beetle she drives has broken down again. But when I called and told her to find another ride, she told me her kid was sick. In short, you're going to be on your own for a while."

"What about the ten-top?"

"Tell your ten-top that they're welcome to have the lobster. Tell them that Himmler will be happy to start boiling them now. Tell Himmler I said so. Now get back out there and hold things together until I can get some more bodies in here."

6:55 a.m. In the time it has taken me to talk to Manager Joe, three more tables have seated themselves on the waitfloor. I deliver menus and silverware setups, and take their drink orders. Then I inform the Wiles party that they are welcome to have the lobster.

"The manager says you're welcome to have the lobster," I say to Mrs. Wiles.

"I thought as much. Your lobster policy is almost as ridiculous and unfair as your attendance policy and grading standards. I plan to have a talk with the head of the Humanities Department at RCCC first thing tomorrow morning." Her smile is diamond-hard. "By the way, we'll all have our eggs scrambled."

6:57 a.m. When I run drinks to my three new tables, they all order the lobster and egg special, eggs scrambled, with buttermilk pancakes as their side orders.

7:02 a.m. I hand the two-pound bag of Aqua Vitae Blend that I set up earlier to Harry the Hippy, who must've slipped in while I was taking my last round of food orders. I take Harry's money and keep his change. Then I hang tickets for all four of the food orders I just took—all at once, with a total of seventeen lobsters, thirty-four scrambled eggs, and thirty-four buttermilk pancakes among them.

Himmler's response consists almost exclusively of the word *fuck*—coupling barnyard animals, vegetables, and assorted kitchen appliances to every imaginable orifice on myself and Manager Joe and our mothers, the customers and their mothers, even the purple pterodactyl and its mother, at a volume which raises the possibility that even the pterodactyl's mother will be able to hear.

7:03 a.m. The effect of Himmler's tirade on the customers is almost exactly the same as the one I observed when the weird keening scream was suddenly cut off during shift change. Everyone in the restaurant pauses. Blinks. Looks around. Even Harry the Hippy—a man who has lived longer and harder, and seen and done more than anyone else in Austin—looks shocked.

"*¡Increíble!*" Harry says, raising an eyebrow and twisting a finger into his braided white beard. "That's going to cost you some tip dollars, my boy."

"If not for my wife and son, my mortgage, and my student loan debt, I'd be saying the same thing."

"I hear you, buddy," Barkeep says. "I work with the public myself. What I always do, when I can't toss a customer out on his ass, is picture him in the most embarrassing scene I can imagine."

"Does it work?" I ask.

"It's always good for a smile."

"Can it, Himmler!" I hear Manager Joe bark, behind me. Then he goes on, much lower: "Why all the negativity toward mothers?"

"This world was built by a loving and perfect God," Himmler says, "that does not accept mothers who won't take *no* for an answer."

"Are you saying you know the mind of God?"

"I'm saying the Apocalypse is near at hand, my friend, and I intend to go out in an orgy of blood and bowel-spurting."

"Find somebody else to insult," Manager Joe says. "Please."

"Who?"

"Anyone but the customers."

"Hey, Himmler," I say. "How about students?"

"Damn straight! Death to all faggot students and their cocksucking counterparts under the desks!"

"Hey, Teacher Joe," Manager Joe snarls at me. "How about giving a little service to your new customers?"

On the waitfloor behind me, I see three new groups of customers in the process of seating themselves, and one that has already self-seated. "I'm on it," I say. Then I look at Harry the Hippy. "Can I get you a cup of coffee, Harry?"

"I've got to go," Harry says. "Problems at home. *Buena suerte*, my boy."

"Thanks, Harry," I say. "Good luck to you, too."

7:15 a.m. I gather up menus, silverware setups, and a coffee pot. But before I head for the waitfloor, I stop back by the bar. "I talked to Manager Joe," I say to Barkeep as I top off his cup. "He says that Annie won't be coming in." Then I make a drink-taking and refilling round. I'm apologizing the whole way, moving from coffee cup to empty coffee cup, trying to smooth the ruffled feathers of mothers and offspring who have not only been insulted by Himmler but also had their coffees run dry.

7:20 a.m. I put together the four new drink orders and make my way back across the restaurant, setting down coffees and icewaters and O.J.'s, and taking breakfast orders as I go.

7:25 a.m. I hang all four new tickets, again all at once, and hear Himmler break into a series of intricate variations on the use of the word *fuck* the likes of which I've never heard. This time, most of them seem to be aimed at waitpeople who hang multiple tickets.

"At least none of them ordered lobster or pancakes!" I say into a break in the string of expletives that comes as Himmler starts to slam plates of steaming lobster, scrambled eggs, and buttermilk pancakes down in the pickup window.

7:30 a.m. As I stack the Wiles order onto two oval trays, Himmler breaks into song. The tune is "Row, Row, Row Your Boat," but the words have been altered:

Kill, kill, kill them all
Kill them all real slow
Shackle them, flay their skin, cut off their balls
Then choke off their airflow

7:32 a.m. To my immense surprise, Manager Joe—who is in the kitchen helping Himmler throw down enough food to fill all of the orders I've just taken—actually starts to sing along.

Then I hear Barkeep take up the song as well.

"What are you still doing here?" I ask Barkeep. "I figured you'd be on your way to Annie's by now."

"Moral support," Barkeep says in a pause between stanzas. "You looked like you could use a dose. Remember to picture them in as embarrassing a scene as you can think of."

I nod, heft both oval trays, and stagger toward the Wiles party.

7:33 a.m. I set the oval trays down on a couple of empty tables and start to serve food, setting lobster and eggs and pancakes down in front of Mrs. Wiles first, and then working my way around the table to end up with her son.

"It's about time," the old woman says, her diamonds flashing.

"Yes, ma'am." I hand out cracking tools and refill coffees, the whole time trying to come up with a scene embarrassing enough to do the job.

7:37 a.m. As I load three more tickets worth of lobster, scrambled eggs, and buttermilk pancakes onto the two oval trays and start back across the waitfloor, I notice that the customers have started to sing Himmler's song—even though it's them Himmler is singing about skinning, castrating, and killing.

7:38 a.m. I check the Wiles table as I pass by, and see that they are all happily chewing and swallowing. They are chewing to the beat of the song.

7:39 a.m. Suddenly, from out of the blue, I picture them as cattle. I imagine the entire Wiles family as a black bald-faced herd, grazing on Bermuda grass and chewing their cuds in the Southwest Texas sun. Then I remember my father—who is probably about to finish pairing up cows and calves right about now—and our long-running dispute about the loyalty versus the stupidity of cattle, and it comes to me that I have been wrong: cattle are not, after all, the stupidest animals on earth.

But just as I decide I'll have to call my father and admit he's right, I look back at Barkeep—who is still sitting there and singing Himmler's song, lending me moral support when he'd rather be seeing Annie—and it comes to me that my father has been wrong about cattle also: they are not the most loyal creatures on earth, either.

7:40 a.m. I serve plates of lobster, scrambled eggs, and buttermilk pancakes to three more tables. Then I take up Himmler's song myself.

For the first time in I don't know how long, I feel myself smile.

I'm Connie Chung

Mayo kills lice. It also conditions your hair. I've been to I've-got-lice-land. I know. Like the great Connie Chung, who traveled the world in 1972 to report on the Nixon/Brezhnev SALT I talks and on Nixon's final trip to the Middle East, I report from experience.

When I got infested in third grade with *piojos* from the nappy head of my ex-best-friend Becky Caluga, Lethy rubbed a whole jar of Kraft Mayonnaise into my hair. I remember the goopy feel of the mayo and Lethy's fingernails like crawdad claws in the mud on my head. I remember thinking my hair would be that way always, a greasy black-and-white ooze like the bottom of Barton Creek between your toes. I remember the big third-grade tears welling up in my eyes and the taste of salt in my mouth and the raspy burn at the back of my throat that came from knowing I would be ugly forever. But Lethy washed out the mayo and combed my hair with a fine-toothed comb. Then she brushed and brushed it, until my hair looked as sleek and shiny-black as the sky full of stars reflected in Barton Springs Pool.

Now Lethy is dead, beaten to death like a dog—*Beyond recognition*, the local CBS anchor said—and I'm out lowriding with my ex-best-friend Becky's brother, Bobby Caluga, looking to capture on videotape the gang-banging *pachuco* who smashed Lethy's face in.

My grandfather, Harry—who says the Calugas are dirty and live like animals, *como animales*, he says—thinks I'm out looking for his antique rocking chair that got stolen off our porch last week. I told Bobby Caluga that we were out looking for Harry's rocker, too. If I'd told Harry and Bobby that I was going out to videotape Mr. Gangster, Harry would've locked me up in the attic bedroom I share with his desk in the corner and the manual typewriter that's all the time getting caught in his crazy beard. And even if I could've escaped, Bobby would never have taken me out this afternoon in his pot-and-breakfast-taco-smelling Ford Falcon to hunt Mr. Gangster down.

In a way, maybe I am out looking for Harry's rocking chair. Harry gets this ice-in-his-intestines feeling every time something terrible is about to happen—the colder the feeling, he says, the worse the bad thing that comes—and he is all the time talking about the blizzard he farted on the night the police came and took away my dad. Well, I've had an ice-cold feeling in my belly all day that the *pachuco* who beat out Lethy's brains and the asshole who boosted Harry's rocker are one and the same. Which is why—and I wasn't fool enough to broadcast this to Harry or Bobby either—in addition to my Sony Camcorder, I came packing heat.

Brains. *Sesos*, Lethy would call them, if she hadn't had her face smashed in. *Sesos* also happens to be Bobby Caluga's nickname. Bobby is as dirty as his sister, Becky; but he drives this phat canary-yellow '64 Ford Falcon, and he's easy to bribe. I got him to ride me and my hot pink backpack—heavy with my camcorder, the senior picture that Lethy took before she dropped out to have me, and the Saturday night special that Daddy hid in the floorboards under my attic bed just as the cops busted in—around South Austin for ten bucks worth of gas and a bag full of Harry's world-famous *tacos de sesos y mayonesa.*

"Hey, *Sesos*," I say. "Turn left on Sacramento."

"*¿Cómo?*" *Sesos* mumbles. His mouth is full of brains and eggs and mayonnaise.

"*¡Doble a la izquierda en Sacramento!*" I say again. "*¡Horita, Sesos!* Dammit, now!"

He whips the chrome chainlink steering wheel around one-handed, and I hear the tires squeal and feel the top edge of the half-open window press into my cheek. We skid sideways, and a pick-up with a black cowcatcher rushes for my face and flashes past as *Sesos* fishtails and then lines the Falcon out onto Sacramento.

"*Boboso*," I say. We don't call *Sesos* "brains" because he's got it going on upstairs. *Tacos de sesos y mayonesa* is *Sesos*'s favorite food, and the nickname comes from him carrying the brains around in his belly instead of his head. He's halfway through the bag of tacos now; and the smell of mayo, combined with the reek of the blunt *Sesos* just smoked, reminds me so much of Lethy and her mayonnaise lice-treatment that I feel like I'm about to barf or cry or both. Even though Lethy was using, and screwing around on Daddy while he was doing time, I believe that she would've been a good mom if she could.

"*¿Hay problema?*" *Sesos* mumbles, his mouth still full.

"Yeah, I got a problem." I'm trying to sound tough, but I can't help sniffling. "You're messing up my grid. I got all 78704 south of Oltorf squared up on this map, remember? We can finish it off before dark if you can dig your head out of your ass."

"Christ, *Cacahuetita*! It's just a freaking rocking chair!" *Sesos* shoots me a major-league *mal de ojo* for as long as it takes him to bite off, chew up, and swallow another mouthful of brains and eggs. "This is just about a freaking rocker, ain't it, *Cacahuetita*?"

It comes to me that *Sesos*, dirty and dumb as he is, has guessed my plan. But I stare straight back into the evil eye he's shooting me, and like the great Connie Chung—who obtained an exclusive interview with Chinese leader Li Peng five years after the massacre at Tiananmen Square—I keep my cool. "Don't call me *Cacahuetita*," I say. "I ain't nobody's Peanut. Not any more. I'm Connie Chung. And I'm going to catch on tape the bastard who stole Harry's rocking chair."

"Okay, okay. *No te cagas*, Connie." He points the evil eye out the window, away from me. "Don't shit.

If you wanna waste your life reading cue cards in front of a camera, *es tu vida*, eh?"

"Connie Chung uses a teleprompter, not cue cards. The *CBS Evening News* ain't *The Late Show with David Letterman*. What you know about broadcast journalism would fit on the head of a roach clip."

"I know that Connie Chung got her ass canned from CBS for telling the world Newt Gingrich called Hillary Clinton a bitch, after Connie promised Gingrich's mom to keep it quiet if the old lady told what Newt said." *Sesos* laughs at that. Then I see his eyes get as big, almost, as his taco-filled belly; and I feel his greasy fingers grab my arm. "That's Harry's rocker right over there!"

"*Mentiroso*," I say.

"No lie!" he says. "It's for sale!"

Sure enough, I catch sight of Harry's rocking chair out the driver's side window. The rocker is closest to the street in a yard full of wooden tables and chairs that look like they've been restored. And sure enough, *SE VENDE*, says a sign in red hand-painted letters tacked up on an oak tree above another sign that says FOR SALE in hand-painted letters that are black.

"I didn't mean *mentiroso* about the rocker," I say. "I meant about Connie Chung. She didn't get fired from CBS over the bitch interview. Connie was made a patsy for the low ratings of her co-anchor, Dan Rather, a man with the camera presence of a piece of wood."

"That ain't what I heard." *Sesos* rides by real slow, makes a U-turn in the next block, then whispers up to the curb with my half-open window so close to Harry's stolen rocker I could reach out and touch it.

Instead I unzip my backpack, snap my camcorder up, and shoot the whole scene—Harry's rocker, the SE VENDE and FOR SALE signs, and the rest of what looks like last-chance-land for stolen-and-restored South Austin. I zoom in on the moon and stars Harry carved into the headrest of the rocking chair the summer my grandmother died. I remember Harry telling *mi abuelita* Dalia that he would rest his head next to hers in the heaven of his own carving until it came time to rest his soul in *el cielo del Señor*. When I snap the camcorder back down into my backpack, I run my hand across the shiny snub-nosed revolver beside it and ask my grandmother for the strength to haul back the hammer if Mr. Gangster dares to show his face.

"Who cares what you heard, *Sesos*?" I ask. "Did you hear that Connie just signed a million-dollar contract with ABC?"

"You can make a million a year doing that newscasting crap?"

"It ain't crap if you're Connie Chung." I leave the backpack unzipped and the door unlocked as *Sesos* and I climb out of the car. Behind the stolen furniture and the tacked-up signs, a couple dozen sets of windchimes hang from the eaves of the house. But there is no wind, and no music, as *Sesos* and I stand on the curb and look at the rocker. Someone has sanded out the scratches and coffee rings, and stained the oak a nice dark red— Harry has this unfortunate thing for blonde wood—and when I run my hand over the moon and stars Harry carved, I can tell the newly-stained surface has been resealed. All the time I'm taking this in, I'm thinking the rocker looks a lot better than it did before it got stolen, and wondering how somebody who could bring back grace to a beautiful object could pound a face into pulp. But then I remember how Harry spent the whole summer my grandmother was dying of cancer carving heaven into the back of that chair for himself and *mi abuelita* to share—and their heaven was supposed to be blonde, not red.

"It looks better," *Sesos* says.

"Just darker," I say.

Then the screen door bangs open, and an old woman weaves her way toward *Sesos* and me. It comes to me that this could be Mr. Gangster's mother, or his grandmother maybe, and I look hard into her face for traces of his. The woman has big, full lips, and her salt-and-pepper hair is kinky like a *negra*, but she has *latina* skin. Mr. Gangster's lips were thin—I'll never forget the way he smiled at my breasts with his hand in Lethy's shorts—and his hair was *pachuco*-clipped. But then I see the same Robert Deniro mole on the old woman's cheek that I saw on Mr. Gangster's, and I feel my belly turn to ice again.

I look from Mr. Gangster's mole on the old woman's face back down at the rocker, feeling the ice grind like a glacier in my belly as the old woman walks up next to *Sesos* and stops. It comes to me that the deep red stain on the wood is the color of blood. And the more I think about the rocker being stolen and then stained the color of the blood Mr. Gangster shed—the blood of Harry and Dalia's daughter-in-law, the blood of my mother—the more I find myself wanting to whip Daddy's pistol out of my backpack and make a smoking hole in the old woman's cheek where Mr. Gangster's Robert Deniro mole used to be.

"May I help you?" the old woman asks after a while.

"We came to see your son," I say, and look up.

I see *Sesos* shoot me another major-league *mal de ojo*. But the old woman's face is pure surprise. She looks me up and down, her eyes wide; and her big, full lips part as she sucks in air. Then she narrows her eyes into mine.

"I'm afraid you've come to the wrong place," she says.

"You're saying you don't have a son?"

"I'm saying my son is dead."

"Then it must be your grandson I'm thinking of," I say without missing a beat.

The *mal de ojo* on *Sesos*'s face and the evil eye on the face of the old woman are now exactly the same.

85

"My grandson is dead to me also," she says, after too long a time for truth-telling.

"How convenient for you," I say. "What about his victims?"

"I don't know what you're talking about."

"No?" Before I know what's happening, I'm inside *Sesos*'s Ford Falcon smelling brains and eggs and mayonnaise as I dig through my backpack. I reach past the camcorder and the spare tape, feeling the gun cold as the ice in my belly. But instead of throwing down on the old woman, I pull out Lethy's senior picture and stick it straight up at that Robert Deniro mole. "I'm talking about Leticia Armazón. I'm talking about my mother."

I'm praying with everything in me for Lethy to reach her nicotine-stained fingers out of Purgatory and tear the face off Mr. Gangster's grandma. Then the evil eye of the old woman softens onto the photo of Lethy I'm holding. She gets a look on her face like maybe her belly has turned to ice, too.

And then, out of nowhere, she says, "Please." She takes a slow breath, and swallows hard. "Please," she says again. "May I?" Then she takes Lethy's picture from my hand.

I rest my empty fingers on the arm of Harry's rocking chair and say nothing at all.

"She's lovely," the old woman says after a while.

"She used to be."

"She must have been a good mother."

"No," I say, remembering the last time I saw Lethy alive. "But she might've changed."

"People sometimes do," the old woman says. "But I've never had any luck trying to change them."

"Did your grandson restore this rocking chair, or did you?"

"Sometimes he brings me broken things," she says, looking hard at the picture. When she looks back at me, her eyes are wet. "I do my best to make them whole again."

"It looks real good," *Sesos* says, in his nicest don't-cry-old-lady voice.

I forgot *Sesos* was even standing there. Running my hand over the rocking chair that the old woman has done her best to restore, studying her eyes that are wet from looking at Lethy, I feel almost as though we are connected—as though Mr. Gangster has made her as much a victim as Lethy or me.

"How long has it been since you saw your grandson?" I ask.

"A long time," the old woman says, after another too-long-for-truth-telling pause. "It's been a very long time."

I snatch Lethy's picture back from her lying hand. "Come on, *Sesos*. We've got a phone call to make."

"Please!" the old woman says. "I'd bring her back if I could. I do the best I can."

I climb into the car, slam the door shut, and snap my camcorder up to shoot the old woman's lying face. But by the time I find the zoom, the car is moving. The only thing I catch is the blood-colored rocking chair, very small in the viewfinder and then gone.

White Rabbit

Here I am, Annie Wild—"Yeah, right," Martin would say; "Annie *Mild* is more like it."—sitting on the back porch and listening to the sound of rain on the roof. I lean back in my rocking chair, smelling the rain as it soaks into my herb garden and savoring the scents of rosemary and oregano and the basil that I set out too early. The basil is sulking in spite the warm May shower, but I'm hoping that the full onset of spring will cheer it into new life.

There is my roommate, Martin Martini—it's not his real name, although he'd never admit that—snoring gently in the rocker next to mine. Even snoring, Martin is the most beautiful man I have ever seen. Lean-muscled, square-jawed, he makes his living modeling outdoor clothing, but wants to be a soap opera star.

There is my son, Crockett—named by his father, who deserted both of us, after one of the last defenders of the Alamo—playing in a mud puddle in the backyard. In his yellow slicker and his bright red galoshes, his hands buried to the wrists in muddy water, he looks so normal and so everyday that it is easy for me to pretend he is just another seven-year-old boy playing in a backyard on another rainy day in Austin.

It's Mother's Day, and after telling Manager Joe that I can't come in to cover the Lobster Brunch shift I picked up, I'm feeling almost cheered into new life myself. I'm relishing the thought that, at least today, I won't be serving pancakes and eggs underneath the purple pterodactyl that hangs like the ghost of a past Apocalypse from the ceiling at Aqua Vitae Café. Instead I'll be heading out later to plant a tree with my son, Crockett, and a guy I've been dating named Barkeep. Barkeep—his real name is Bryan, but he prefers the nickname—is a bartender, of course; and he is generous with draft beer, which is handy considering my financial circumstances. But the best thing about Barkeep is that, unlike any other guy I've ever been out with, he's great with my son. Barkeep is nowhere near as beautiful as Martin, though, who is also great with Crockett, and who has graced the covers of J. Crew and L.L. Bean.

But then again, I am nowhere near as beautiful as Martin, either. And I've got Crockett, who sends most men into full retreat at first sight. As Martin himself is so fond of saying, "Beggars can't be choosers." I plan to lure Barkeep back here after the tree-planting with promises of homebrew, and then put Crockett down for a nap. The drum of rain on the roof and the smell of herbs from the garden lull me into a waking dream that features the gray-frosted carpet of Barkeep's chest hair, his bulky ex-Airborne muscles, and the scent of sweat on his sun-freckled skin.

Beside me, Martin suddenly snorts, springs out of his own rocker, and screams, "Holy shit!" Despite his soap opera hysterics and the fact that he's gay, he is more attractive to me at this moment than Barkeep will ever be, even in dreams.

I am still half-asleep. In my waking dream, where bulky and freckled Bryan is beginning to take on Martin's lean musculature and deep tan—but of course staying beer-generous, Crockett-friendly Barkeep in every other way—I see Crockett squeeze through a gap in the back fence with a rabbit clutched tightly in his hands. It is a white rabbit. The white rabbit looks very dead.

"Holy shit!" Martin says again. "Do you see that?"

"Please don't say that you see it, too."

Martin says nothing. But there is Crockett—grinning at me the way only a 140-pound autistic seven-year-old can grin—climbing onto the porch and laying the dead white rabbit at my feet.

"Bunny," Crockett says. "Easter Bunny, Annie."

"God," I say. "Oh God. It's Elsie's Easter rabbit. She must have left it out in the backyard."

"Are you freaking out yet?" Martin asks. "I am."

Here I am trying hard not to freak out as I relive the memory of Elsie and her Easter rabbit, just a few short weeks ago, playing dress-up in the backyard next door. In my memory the bright April sun shines on the rabbit that is as white as Elsie's Easter dress, and on the pink ribbons around its neck that are the same color as the bow in Elsie's hair. The rabbit's eyes—half-open now, and glazed the color of blood—are, in my memory, that same Easter-bow pink.

"If you're not freaking out, you should be," Martin says. "Because Kenny is going to freak out enough for both of us. He's going to freak out completely."

At the sound of Kenny's name, Crockett moans low in this throat. And I get a vision, an end-of-the-world flashforward as vivid as my Easter flashback, of Kenny finding out that Crockett has killed his daughter's bunny. I see Kenny's neck bulge, see the veins in his eyes go varicose with the spike in his blood pressure as he screams that Crockett has violated the court order for the last time—and that he is going to haul Crockett and me into court and have my son taken away from me.

"I will not freak out," I say. "I am woman. I am invincible."

But despite the resolute words of Helen Reddy's best and most uplifting song, I feel myself losing my shit completely. Crockett really has just violated a court order—Kenny's court order, protecting Kenny's rights as a property owner from the depredations of the "destructive and uncontrolled" autistic boy next door. As though the backyard fence wasn't falling apart. As though our landlord—a possessor of property rights himself—hadn't refused to pay to have the fence replaced. As though non-property-owners don't have the right to backyard fences without holes. As though Crockett, autistic or not, doesn't have the right to be a boy.

"I take it back," Martin says. "Kenny won't freak out. He'll explode. I warned you about that kid messing around next door."

"So did Kenny," I half-snarl, half-sob. "Crocket must've slipped through the fence while I was napping. Would you like to scream at me, too?"

"I would if I were Kenny," Martin says. Hearing Crockett moan again, he leans down and says, "Kenny, Kenny, Kenny."

Crockett raises his fist and yells fiercely in the direction of the run-down three-bedroom ranch-style house next door.

Here I am wondering what it is about men that makes them so *male*. Not even gays and autistic boys are immune. I mean, here is Martin, Mr. Catalog Cover—who had dates last month with more men than I've been out with in my whole life—taking the side of the homophobic NRA posterboy next door who wants to use a court order to have my son taken away from me. And here is Crockett, *male* through and through—even though, at seven years old, he has the mental faculties of a toddler—snatching up Elsie's Easter bunny and shaking it in his fist like a stuffed toy.

"You're not going to side with that asshole," I say, snatching the rabbit away from Crockett and shaking it in Martin's fashion-model face. "You're going to side with me."

"Sorry, sweetie. This time you and Crockett are on your own."

"If you don't help me right now, I'll tell every one of your boyfriends that it isn't really you on the covers of J. Crew and L.L. Bean."

"They would know it was a lie," Martin says, soap-opera smug.

"Then I'll tell them your real name is Marty Fry-rear."

Here I am standing next to Martin Martini—whose real name truly is Marty Fryrear—as he washes Elsie's dead bunny with his pricey shampoo, blow-dries the dead bunny with his multi-speed and multi-temp hair dryer, then brushes the dead bunny's fur with his silver-backed brush. When Martin finally finishes up his styling session, the dead rabbit looks as though it has just been prepped for a fashion-photo shoot. I push its eyes shut, and the illusion of life is almost perfect.

"It looks alive," I say. But when I take my hand away, the eyelids open again.

"Not with those zombie eyes it doesn't," Martin says.

I push the eyes closed again. I take my hand away. This time the eyelids open in blood-colored slits, as though the Easter Bunny has come back to life stoned out of its mind.

"Do you have any Super Glue?" I ask.

"I think so," Martin says. "But I'm not touching that zombie bunny again. So don't even bother asking me to glue those nasty eyes shut."

"Marty Fryrear," I say, "I'm going to ask you to do more than that."

Here I am, Annie Wild—and this time, even Martin would have to say that the *Wild* fits me as well as the clothes he wears on catalog covers fit him—standing next to Marty Fryrear as he credit-cards open Kenny's sliding glass door. Inside, the run-down three-bedroom ranch smells of deep-fried food and gun oil.

We slip quietly through the kitchen and down a hallway covered with framed collages of Kenny with his thick neck and his comb-over; of his wife, Janie, with her bleach-blonde hair and the big dark sunglasses that almost hide the marks Kenny sometimes leaves on her face; and of Elsie with her bright blue eyes and gap-toothed smile. For a moment, seeing that smile—completely innocent of her daddy's automatic-weapon-toting, beat-the-weak mentality—I falter at the door to Elsie's bedroom, and actually think of turning back.

But then I remember Kenny's court order, and the fact that Crockett's life with me—his entire world, and mine, too—is riding my shoulders. So I walk into Elsie's room with its pink-and-white canopy bed and its matching pink-and-white bedroom suite, place the rabbit back into its cage, and run like hell. We both run like hell, Martin and me, stopping only to slide the patio door shut behind us.

Back inside our own house again, I check on Crockett, who I left watching *The Little Mermaid* on our bedroom TV. He lies quietly on the bed, totally absorbed in his favorite movie. Martin wishes me luck and then flees in his red MG, leaving me to face the possible fallout—Martin calls it "The Kenny Apocalypse"—alone. It seems like I have spent my whole adult life trying to fight Armageddon single-handed. I try calling Barkeep, who took the day off so that we could plant our tree, and have some time together afterwards. But he isn't home, and he's not due here for another hour. So I lock Crockett in the bedroom with *The Little Mermaid*, and slip out onto the back porch with just a homebrew for company to await the return of the neighbors.

A couple of homebrews later, I hear the roar of Kenny's SUV, closely followed by the screech of his automatic garage door that has needed oiling since I can remember. A long silence settles in the wake of the SUV's passing. The rain has stopped now, and the only sound is the slow drip of water from the eaves.

Then the silence is broken by the sound of Kenny's sliding glass door. I hear the stomp of Kenny's boots on his back porch, followed by the rustle of briquets in Kenny's barbeque grill, followed in turn by the splash of the chemical accelerants Kenny uses to make his fire burn quicker and hotter. Then comes the sound of running feet and a voice much too bright and breathless to be Kenny's.

"Daddy, Daddy, the Easter Bunny has been born again!"

"Huh?"

"Look! The Easter bunny has been born again! See? He's a little sleepy, though. I can't get him to open his eyes."

There comes a long pause, followed by the whoosh of Kenny's fire exploding to life inside the grill. The flames leap so high I can see them through the gaps in the backyard fence. "Annie!" I hear Kenny yell. "You crazy bitch! What kind of freak would be sick enough to dig up a dead rabbit and put him back in the cage?"

"Jesus," I hear someone say. "Jesus Christ." The voice sounds like mine, but I don't remember speaking.

I hear the crash of Kenny's patio door slamming shut, followed by the tinkle of glass shattering onto concrete, and I know that the Apocalypse Martin predicted is finally coming to pass. The end of my world is coming. It is almost here.

Electric Truth

I am the Prophet Mudcat. I am the one who sings of love. Listen to my siren song, and recall the perfect and delicious senses you have forgotten how to use.

Consider this. A man who has been blind his whole life wakes up in the middle of the night and discovers that he has been given the gift of sight. He looks at his wife for the first time, quicksilver beside him in the light of a virgin moon; and he realizes that up until this moment, he has been in exile—cast alone into a white-hot desert of unseeing air. Then his wife opens her eyes. He sees himself reflected in the liquid moonlight there, and he learns what it means to be welcomed home.

Come and be received back into the living water.

Turn away from the light of day and embrace cool darkness. Turn your back on thin air and return to the moonlit depths of the water, where your senses can mend.

I will show you how to see, once again, beneath the surface of things. I will teach you to taste again the electric truth contained in each and every touch. You will learn to smell out, once more and forever, the subtle sulfurous perfume which pervades all lies.

Come and be reborn.

Your return will be as effortless as the ebb and flow of tides. Not at all like my own. I had to fight my way back, against the awful power of those who control the air.

As I stood on Congress Avenue, lost in the wonders of the world to come that were being revealed by my newly-expanded senses, I caught the distant hum of helicopter rotors and snapped back into the here and now.

The salamanders said: The Air Force assassins are headed your way.

I ducked underneath an awning, plastered myself against a plate glass window, and listened to the hum of distant rotors balloon into a roar. The awning whipped and buckled as the downdraft passed overhead. But if the assassins had seen me, they showed no sign. Instead, they headed northeast in a slow-spiraling search pattern centered on Town Lake.

The salamanders said: Wait . . . Wait . . . Now go!

I turned right off Congress, ducked left down an alley behind a hardware store, and scaled a wooden privacy fence. On the far side of the fence, a set of steps led up onto a wooden porch stuck onto the back of the junkiest house I'd ever seen. There looked to be room for me underneath. I jumped down, waded through the trash in the narrow dirt yard, and slithered under the stairs.

I had to feel my way in. The crawlspace was cramped and completely black, but surprisingly clean compared to the backyard. The hard-packed dirt floor had been swept clear of debris, and there was no smell of dog. I lay flat on my back in the cool darkness and breathed, prepared for the kind of power nap that would put Rip Van Winkle to shame. But before I could so much as shut my eyes, the porchlight flashed on. Bars of light blazed between the porchboards, and I cut my eyes away into the yard. Then a door banged open, a pair of steel-toed workboots pounded out onto the planks, and a bass voice exploded above my head.

Mr. Steel-toes said: Stick it up your ass!

He stomped down the steps, sending aluminum cans and plastic containers thudding like buckshot against the privacy fence as he kicked and cursed his way across the yard. Then he whirled to face the pair of Birkenstock sandals that came slapping out behind him onto the porch.

Mr. Birkenstocks said: Don't leave! I didn't mean that the way it came out!

As my eyes adjusted to the floodlight on the porch, Mr. Steel-Toes came clear. He was big—at least six-foot four and broad-shouldered—and his bulging arms were covered with tattoos.

Mr. Steel-Toes said: Of course you did, dude. Set one sandal on those fucking steps, and I'll shove a boot up your elevator shaft.

I heard the porchboards creak as Mr. Birkenstocks backed away from the stairs.

Mr. Birkenstocks said: Himmler! Wait! Let's sit down on the steps and pass a peace pipe. We can work out a deal. How about it? I give you total amnesty, plus all the pot you can smoke, and you come back inside and finish your shift.

Himmler said: I have a better idea, dude. You promote me to line cook starting tomorrow, plus find another dishwasher for the rest of tonight; and I don't quit the restaurant right now—and quit your lame Grateful Dead cover band, too.

Mr. Birkenstocks said: You'd quit the band?

Mr. Steel-Toes said: Faster than you can say *"Sugar Magnolia" sucks even worse with no drums to prop its tired ass up.*

Mr. Birkenstocks said: Okay, Himmler. You win. Come back tomorrow ready to train.

Himmler said: Yes!

Then he whirled around in a storm of cans, and kicked his way out the back gate.

The slamming of the back gate was followed by a long pause, during which I heard Mr. Birkenstocks sigh—and during which every bone in my exhausted and mostly-naked body willed Mr. Birkenstocks to go back inside and turn off that light. But he lit a joint instead. And before I could think to do anything at all, Mr. Birkenstocks slapped his way down the steps and crawled into my lap.

We screamed at exactly the same moment, straight into each other's faces, so close I caught a contact buzz off his breath. Then we rolled in opposite directions and came up squinting at each other through the cloud of dust our mad scramble had raised.

Mr. Birkenstocks said: Where the hell did you come from?

I said: Well, I was running through the alley back there and—

He said: Bullshit! You're a spy for Jen and Barry. Jesus! The owners of this dump have even got eyes underneath the cafe.

I said: No, really. I'm trying to hide from spies myself. Air Force assassins, actually. They've got a helicopter and an infrared scanning device.

We were maybe three feet apart, on our hands and knees, trying to read each other's intentions in the play of light and dark and dust. A bar of porchlight slashed across Mr. Birkenstocks's nose and down one pale cheek. I saw his bloodshot brown eyes widen a bit as they took in the rest of me, then I saw the wild look on his face start to fade. He eased down on one elbow, relit the joint, and reached it my way.

Mr. Birkenstocks said: Go ahead and take the whole thing. You look like you need it worse than me.

I said: No thanks. The computer firm I write code for does random drug tests.

He said: Look, I don't know what loony bin you just busted out of, and I don't give a damn. As a matter of fact, this is your lucky day. You can hide here for as long as you want to—just as long as you do what I say.

I said: I won't wash dishes.

He said: You a talented drummer with a thing for the Dead?

I said: Not that I know of.

He said: Then you're washing dishes, dude. Or I'm turning you in.

The salamanders said: Kill this man. Kill him right now.

I said: Do what?

Mr. Birkenstocks said: How hard can this be? You wash dishes, I hide you out. That means if those Air Force guys come around in their helicopter, I'll make them fly away. Same deal for the guys with the funny white jackets, or the cops. You don't wash dishes, I drop a dime on your ass.

The salamanders said: This man is going to hand you over to the authorities. Do you know what that means? The future of your species demands that he die!

I said: That's just not good enough!

Mr. Birkenstocks said: Okay, okay. I'll throw in free food and a set of clean clothes. But that's my final offer. What do you say?

The salamanders said: Kill him now!

I said: What if I told you I was the Prophet of Love on a mission to save the human race?

Mr. Birkenstocks said: You can walk on water when the dishes are done. Now make up your mind, I've got a restaurant to run.

The salamanders said: Run Terminate.exe.

I got a pop-up how-to diagram in my head, all of a sudden, of me snapping Mr. Birkenstocks's neck—a three-step virtual action sequence complete with sound effects. I saw exactly where I should place my hands. I felt the exact amount of force to exert. I heard the sickening crackle of vertebrae that accompanies a 180-degree head-twist. I smelled the potsmoke escaping his virtual lungs as he wheezed his simulated last breath. The effect was so powerful, it was almost impossible to resist. I had to lock my arms tight across my chest to keep from clamping my hands around Mr. Birkenstocks's throat.

I said: Quick! What's your name?

He said: Manager Joe.

99

I said: I'll wash your dishes, Manager Joe. Let's move!

We crawled out and climbed onto the porch. Then Manager Joe swung open the back door, and a hot breath of what my new catfish senses identified as boiling innards washed over us like a wet belch.

He said: Preproom! This is the preproom, dude!

The room he led me into was crammed so full of stainless steel tables, whole fruits and vegetables in boxes, metal appliances, pans on hooks, racks of spices, and upside-down pots stacked on shelves that we had to work our way through single-file. The only other person in sight was a skeletal redhead of indeterminate sex who stood in a corner, stirring a vat full of steaming entrails that I identified now as the source of the stench. Some mysterious something—maybe low blood sugar, maybe the strain of fighting the not-entirely-virtual urge to snap Manager Joe's neck—had shifted my hybrid senses into hyperdrive. The air was pregnant with the flavor of cayenne, black pepper, and oregano. I tasted the raw airborne essence of the freshly-chopped garlic, onions, and peppers that lay in white, yellow, and red mounds next to the stainless steel cauldron. Then I saw the Sexless Redhead scoop a ladleful of gray goo out of the soup vat, and blow the steam straight at me.

The scent was disgusting. It was repulsive. It was so difficult to resist. To my absolute horror, I felt myself starting to salivate. Even worse, I had an overwhelming urge to smear gray goo all over my body. I felt like a fecaphile in the grip of a relapse—hang-dog, humiliated, a hot rocket in my pants.

I said: Salamanders!

The Sexless Redhead said: This here's duck gut gumbo. Ain't no salamander in it.

She or he slurped the entire contents of the ladle and smacked them open-mouthed, like gray intestinal gum. Then he or she met my gaze, gulped with gusto, and grinned with goo-beglobbed teeth.

The salamanders said: Forget the hippy. Kill the sous-chef. It would be a *cause celebre* for waterfowl planetwide.

I couldn't catch my breath. For an eternal moment the only things in existence were innard-splotched incisors, the air thick with guts and spices, and the eager tingling of my tongue. Then I felt a wave of nausea, followed by an even bigger wave of relief at feeling nauseated, which was followed in turn by a cleansing tide of dry heaves.

Catching hold of myself, I chased Manager Joe's backlength black braid around two tight corners and down a narrow throughway to the edge of what looked like an indoor swamp. Ahead of me, two piles of slime-covered dishes rose out of twin over-flowing sinks. The floor was a bog of liquid food mud.

Manager Joe said: This is the dishpit, dude! Consider it your new home.

I said: Dishpit? This place is a cesspool.

As if in agreement, the overloaded and slime-covered dishwashing machine farted a foul-smelling fog.

Manager Joe said: You'll be giving the whole place a spring-cleaning when the dishes are done. Now wade on in, the water's fine.

I tiptoed barefoot into the foodbog that rose to my ankles; and while Manager Joe barked orders, I trained to work the dishpit. I learned how to use the metal soakerhose to pre-squirt the worst of the slime off the glasses and plates and pots and pans and silverware. I learned how to line them up on black plastic dish-racks, roll the loaded racks into the dishmachine, slam the door shut to start the cycle, and go back to pre-squirting slime. When a cycle ended, the dishmachine shut down. Then I lifted the door, rolled the clean dishrack onto the drying table, shoved another dirty dishrack into the dishmachine, slammed the door shut, and pre-squirted more slime.

Manager Joe said: Way to acquire dishwashing skills, dude. Faster! Faster!

I went faster, faster.

He said: Now pick up that soap jug and pour some dishwashing liquid into the hopper!

I picked up the soap jug and poured pale pink dishwashing liquid into the clear plastic container under the dishmachine.

He said: Now go! Go!

I went, went.

He said: You think you got it?

I thought I had it.

He said: You're the most promising rookie scum-scraper I've ever seen. Any questions?

I said: Just one. Is your first name really *Manager*?

He said: What the hell does that have to do with anything?

I said: Humor the scum-scraper.

He said: My first name is Joe.

I said: Is your last name *Manager*?

He said: No.

I said: Then I don't get it. Why *Manager Joe*?

He said: That's more than one question.

I said: But only one subject. Come on.

He said: Okay, three reasons. First, to separate myself from the unwashed, underfed, and freakish—like you. Second, there are two other Joes that work here—Joe Teacher Joe, and Joe the Lead Singer of the Pixels Joe—and those dudes are lame. And third, so you always remember who gives the orders around here—and who scrapes the scum. Now get back to work. And don't forget that spring-cleaning. You'll have to make this dishpit sparkle before you get any food or clean clothes.

Finally, Manager Joe went to give orders to others among the ranks of the unwashed, underfed, and freakish, and I got down to the business of scraping scum. I worked my way through the piles of dishes in both sinks—pre-squirt, stack, roll, slam, pre-squirt, lift, roll, shove, slam, and pre-squirt—losing myself in the rhythm, thinking of nothing but fresh-cooked food and clean, dry clothes. From time to time a girl with blue Chinese characters tattooed on her face and arms came in and took the racks of cleaned and dried dishes away. After a while she brought the racks back empty, and stacked them upside-down on a shelf.

Once I'd finished cleaning the dishes out of both sinks, I drained the foul sinkwater that had been over-flowing into the foodbog, scrubbed out both stainless-steel basins, and refilled them with pink soapy water and clean white suds. Then I started on the dishes that were stacked in dirty black bustubs on the front wall of shelves.

The sixteen shelves—four free-standing wire racks of four shelves each that separated the dishpit from the long throughway Manager Joe had led me down when we came in—held two bustubs apiece. The thirty-two bustubs were completely filled with glasses and plates and pots and pans and silverware, all of which was slathered with another swampful of instant foodmud. As dishwasher, it was my job to add water. There were pots and pans caked with black burnt stuff. There were plates plastered with a yellow-green food-cement made of congealed bacon grease and the dried yokes of fried eggs. There were glasses and coffee cups that had been used for ashtrays.

The salamanders said: So why didn't you kill him?

I said: Kill who?

They said: Manager Joe. Whom else? Why is he not dead? Our pop-up virtual help window should have walked you through his termination step-by-step.

I said: It very nearly did.

They said: Exactly how close would you say you had come?

I said: What do you mean?

They said: On a scale of one to ten—where ten represents a strong urge to eradicate, and one represents no urge at all—how would you rate the strength of your virtual urge to terminate Manager Joe?

I said: I'd give it an eight.

They said: So low? What about the danger he poses to your mission? What about the primal human urge to kill? The man clearly has character issues, and he threatened you. Besides, if you had killed him, you would have avoided this trial by sewer.

I said: I thought you said we were on a mission of peace. Besides, I've got a brilliant plan.

They said: So it was your sense of the mission as peaceful, combined with the existence of an alternative to violence, that kept you from snapping Manager Joe's neck?

I said: Exactly. Now will you please hear me out? Like I said, I've got a brilliant plan. Let's say, hypothetically, that instead of pink soap, I poured this vial full of trendone I've been carrying all night into the hopper on that dishmachine. Would the trendone not coat all the pots and pans and plates and cups and silverware? Would the trendone not work its way into the digestive systems of the eaters and drinkers who dirtied each dish? Would the trendone not spread across Austin in the bodily fluids of those eaters and drinkers, and then on out into the unsuspecting world?

The salamanders said: In short, *no, no, no,* and *of course not.*

I said: What's the problem? Some kind of heat-related hormone breakdown? An RNA reaction with the soap?

They said: The rinse cycle on the dishwashing machine.

I said: Oops.

They said: Colloquial, but correct. In the future, for the sake of the mission, we suggest that you focus your attention on physical tasks and cede all planning duties to a species with more highly-evolved cognitive tools.

I nodded at the row of tea and coffee urns that lined the far wall, across the walkway from the dishpit.

I said: What does a species with more evolved cognitive tools think would happen if I dumped trendone into those beverage vats over there?

They said: Hmm . . .

I said: It's a brilliant plan. Admit it. It should be easy enough to say, even for a species with amphibian lips. Come on . . . *Brill-yant. P-lan.*

They said: Promising, perhaps. But brilliant? We will have to run a series of successful virtual simulations before we are ready to go that far.

I said: While you're at it, let's get something straight. If you ever try to use that virtual reality urge to make me kill someone again, I'll turn myself in.

When I finally finished scraping the scum off the last of the dirty dishes in the last dirty bustub, I took a carving knife and cut through the clog of foodcement that was plugging the drain in the dishpit floor. Once most of the swampwater had been sucked out of the foodbog, I got down on my hands and knees, and started to scrub. I scraped and lathered and bleached and rinsed until all that was left under the dishpit sinks were one slime-coated half-catfish body and a six-by-ten foot swath of glistening concrete. I took a long last look at the job I'd done, then I went to find the megalomaniac in charge of dispensing hot food and clean clothes.

I tracked down Manager Joe in a closet-sized office that opened onto the preproom. Two bare bulbs in the ceiling blazed down on the built-in desk-and-shelf combination that occupied most of the room. The walls were lined from floor to ceiling with shelves filled with hundreds of CD's. On the desk sat a state-of-the-art sound system and the battered Birkenstocks of Manager Joe. His waistlength black braid whipped around when I knocked on the open door, and he narrowed his eyes at me.

Manager Joe said: You don't smell so good, dude. And you don't look so good either.

I said: I just reclaimed a swamp single-handed, and I can't remember the last time I had solid food.

He said: So you got that dishpit knocked out?

I said: Dishes sparkling, concrete glistening.

He said: We'll see about that. But just in case, how do you like your eggs?

I asked for as many as he thought the job was worth, sunny side up, with a short stack of buttermilk pancakes on the side. He came back about fifteen minutes later with a half-dozen eggs, two plate-sized pancakes, and enough maple syrup to re-plug the dishpit drain. He put it all down on the desk next to the stereo, along with a tall glass of milk, and invited me to sit and eat.

Manager Joe said: Sparkling and glistening is right. Go ahead and fuel up. Then we'll hose you down and get you a set of clean clothes.

I sat at the desk and savored pancakes and eggs in a way I that wouldn't have believed possible, if it hadn't been happening in my own mouth. I was chewing and swallowing just like always. But the whole time my teeth were doing the same old thing, the salty tang of eggs and the sweet rich tastes of buttermilk pancakes and maple syrup were holding a *menage a trois* on my hybridized tastebuds. It felt a lot like the reaction I'd had to the smell of duck-gut gumbo when I first walked in the preproom door—only more intense.

I felt myself actually catching some kind of bizarre foodbuzz.

The more I chewed and swallowed, the more the magnitude of the sensory shockwaves shooting back and forth between my brain and my tongue seemed to build. I wolfed both plates of breakfast food without even pausing to take a drink of milk. When the last of the eggs and pancakes had been eaten, I found myself face-down over the desk, licking the syrup off my plate.

I said: Salamanders! What the hell is happening to me?

The salamanders said: Your hominid heredity appears to be rearing its ugly head.

I said: Hominid, hell. This feels like a catfish thing.

They said: How so?

I explained about the breakfast food buzz, the *menage a trois* on my tongue, my overwhelming desire earlier to smear boiled duck guts on my skin.

The salamanders said: The sensory episodes you have described are most likely a result of your evening exertions—a series of powerful endorphin bursts, a sort of syncopated runner's high.

I said: This is way too intense a buzz to have come from exercise. I got marijuana poisoning once from doing three-liter gravity bong hits with hashish. This feels a lot like that, except my mouth is drier and there's more of a crust on my tongue.

They said: Poisoning is a possibility. You may have been exposed to harmful chemicals in the lake. Pesticides, most likely, or fertilizer runoff.

I said: You mean Town Lake is polluted with toxic chemicals?

They said: Virtually every body of water on your cesspool of a planet is tainted with one toxin or another. Those DON'T EAT THE FISH signs under the bridges were not posted for fun.

I said: Now that you mention it, I do have a funny taste in my mouth. But it doesn't taste chemically. It tastes more like . . . I don't know. Like the way a bathroom smells . . .

In my hybridized mind's eye, all of a sudden, I saw the water treatment plant. In my virtual vision, the plant was spewing raw sewage into the water I'd been breathing since the night of my sea change.

I said: Oh my God!

They said: Calm yourself. The water treatment plant you worked in until tonight is perfectly safe. This tongue crust. What does it taste like, exactly?

I said: Would you like me to rate the strength of its rankness on a scale of one to ten?

They said: We would like you to be more specific in your use of descriptive terms. Is there an air of fecundity? Just a hint of the stuff of life?

I said: It tastes like shit.

The salamanders said: Then it may be the trendone.

I said: Go upgrade a new love prophet. I quit.

They said: What about the future of your species?

I said: Screw my species. I'm out of here.

They said: No, wait! Perhaps the problem is not the trendone alone. It could be interacting with something. We will run a series of virtual simulations, ASAP, and inform you the moment we get the results.

I said: What the hell am I supposed to do in the meantime?

They said: Sleep.

I said: Sleep? That's it?

They said: A stretch of uninterrupted slumber should give your upgraded system time to purge itself of any toxins you might have picked up in your flight through the lake. But first, we strongly suggest a bath.

Just then Manager Joe stuck his head in the office door and strongly suggested the same thing. He took me back to the dishpit and squirted me down with the soakerhose while I stood in the sink. Finally, he tossed me the set of clean clothes he'd promised—a pair of white cotton pants, a white cotton shirt, and a white cotton apron to go over both—and headed for the office, leaving me standing there in my Speedo with an armload of clean clothes and a bare foot in each sink.

I said: Hey! What about shoes?

He said: That wasn't part of our deal, dude. But I might be willing to sweeten my offer. If you promise to stick around for tomorrow, I'll throw in a pair of workboots for tomorrow night's shift. How does that sound?

I said: Not sweet enough.

He said: Okay, okay. I'm in a giving mood. Along with the workboots, I'll bring you a pair of clean socks. And I'll even let you crash in the office tonight when you're done cleaning up.

I said: I'm your new dishwasher, Manager Joe. Let's move.

I limped into the office, piled some kitchen clothes in a corner, and collapsed. Neither the incandescent glare of twin bare bulbs nor the lingering stink of duck-gut gumbo could stand between me and sleep. But as I drifted into unconsciousness, I heard distant and familiar whispers at the back of my mind.

The salamanders said: Remember, Prophet Mudcat. Yesterday is only today's memory; but tomorrow is today's dream. And all dreams lie in the realm of the fifth dimension.

I said: Hmm . . . ?

They said: Think of the fifth dimension as a bubble. Or rather, as a chain of bubbles that is intricately interconnected and contains all things vital to the human heart. Each bubble holds a field of dunes at the edge of a deep blue sea, and each dune is driven forward by the ocean breeze. Think of the windward side of each dune as the present moment and each slip-face as the future. Think of every action taken in the name of love as a grain of sand swirling up the back of each space-time wave and over onto the slip-face of the future, which is thereby changed for the good. In the age to come, if you accomplish your mission, your world will be a waking dream of love . . .

So I sing you this siren song, my soon-to-be brothers and sisters, as I drift through fifth-dimensional dreams of love. Come and dream with me.

Together, we will make those dreams come true.

Love Grudge

From: superchicopal@yahoo.com
To: jjasmine@riverccc.edu
Cc: monalisa@brightok.net
Subject: HUM 1613

Dear Dr. Jasmine:

You might not remember me, since I've missed as many of your classes as I've been to, but my name is Opal Rogers and I'm writing to ask you to let me to withdraw from your Classic Civ course with a grade of W instead of an F. As I believe I have the best possible excuse for all twelve absences, I hope you'll read this letter with an open heart and an open mind. You may even get a laugh out of it, as has everyone involved except for Mona.

It all started when I was in 8th grade back in Broken Bow, Oklahoma. Mamma and Daddy got this love grudge going where they'd split up for a couple months and then get back together and move to a new town. The way they would get back together was this: Daddy would track Mamma down wherever it was she'd run off to, and over a couple of days worth of making up in some cheap hotel or other, he would talk her into coming back. Then they'd pick up stakes, head a little farther west, and start fresh. They wound up dragging us across half of Oklahoma because they couldn't decide whether they wanted to be together or beat each other up. They had blow-ups in Broken Bow, Antlers, and Durant—followed by shack-ups in New Orleans, Dallas, and Kansas City, MO—before they finally cooled their jets in Ardmore long enough for me to get my GED.

I moved to Austin in January and enrolled in classes at RCCC, including your Classic Civ course. I remember you assigned us that really cool poem about the king who earned the love of a goddess that he impressed by killing a monster and chopping down a tree. The king's name was Gilgamesh and the goddess's name was Ishtar. I forget the name of the monster and the tree.

Anyway, I moved in with my boyfriend, a real cutie who moved from Ardmore to Austin to play bass in a band, and things were going great for the two of us. Then about a month later, Mamma showed up at our house and told me that she'd left Daddy again, and asked could she sleep on our couch for a couple days. It was okay by me, but the first thing Derrick said was, "She can't crash here." Derrick is my boyfriend. The band he plays bass in is The Pixels, and they've got a hot new single out right now called "Rainbow Tattoo" that you can hear on 107.1 KGSR.

Well, I told Derrick that if Mamma couldn't stay with us until she got her feet back underneath her, I'd stop work on the big new tattoo I've been adding onto bit by bit— it's the inspiration for the hit song Derrick wrote—and we'd stop doing all the things that he liked so much and that we'd been doing pretty much non-stop since I moved in. That got Derrick's attention, I guess. So Mamma slept on our couch that night, and the next day she went and got her a cashier job at Artz Rib House here in South Austin. This was good not only because it got Mamma off the couch, but also because she could walk to Artz, which is right down the street from our house.

Things couldn't have been going any better for Mamma and Derrick and me. Mamma was no trouble at all because she was gone all the time, Derrick and me were enjoying each other's company even more than we'd done before, work on my new tattoo—a beautiful six-colored arc that stretches all the way from the front to the back of me—was coming along slowly but surely, and I was going to all my classes, including yours. I remember we'd gotten to the part of the poem where King Gilgamesh refuses to marry Ishtar, and Ishtar is so heartbroken about her love being contempted that she sends a giant bull to show King Gilgamesh the terrible power of a woman scorned.

Then, just like King Gilgamesh, things for Mamma and Derrick and me took a turn for the worst. First, Daddy got him a girlfriend named Mona. Then he called me to ask if it was okay for him to take Mona out on dates. I said, "Personally, I don't think it's right, you still being married to Mamma and all."

He said, "Ain't your Mamma been goin' out?" Well, I made the mistake of admitting how Mamma was spending most every night out at The Broken Spoke, dancing and getting drunk and not coming home much. And the next night—that would be the night after the last day I attended your class—Daddy showed up to bring Mamma all her stuff. He also brought his new girlfriend, Mona, who he proceeded to tell Mamma was named after a painting. Then he said how much prettier a picture Mona was than the one he'd been staring at for the past twenty years.

As you might expect, the fight started just about the time Daddy got done running his mouth. Well, I guess there were three fights in all—Mamma and Mona, Mona and me, and Daddy and Derrick. Mamma said she was gonna show Mona what you get when you mess around with a married man, then she shoved Mona in the chest so hard Mona's blouse got ripped. Mona responded by knocking out Mamma, who was drunk—having just come back from The Broken Spoke alone for a change—

and then I heaved Mona down the front steps so hard that she broke her left leg and ruptured her spleen. When Daddy went to hit me for heaving Mona, Derrick laid him out next to Mamma with one punch. It was the second fight I'd seen Daddy in with anybody other than Mamma, and the second time I'd seen him knocked cold.

Pretty soon the police showed up, and I got charged with felony assault because of the injuries to Mona, who I last saw being loaded into the back of an ambulance and carted off to emergency surgery. Derrick, who was charged with simple assault, was so mad at me that he wouldn't pay for me a lawyer or even post my bail. Mamma, who was also charged with felony assault, lost her job at Artz Rib House for missing work and couldn't afford to bail herself out, much less me. So I wound up spending a month in the county jail—where I couldn't eat or sleep, and spent my nights thinking about how King Gilgamesh missed out on living forever because he couldn't stay awake and then missed his chance at a making a fresh start in life because that snake ate the plant he found at the bottom of the sea. To make a long story short, this is also why I got the twelve absences in your Classic Civ class.

In case you're curious, Mamma and Daddy got back together, as usual. Daddy came down to the jailhouse last weekend to serve Mamma with divorce papers, and they spent visiting hours talking about how much they had been missing each other since they split up. First thing Monday morning, Daddy bailed Mamma out and drove her over to the Days Inn; and after a couple days of making it all up to each other, they moved to San Angelo. Daddy says he's left Mona, Oklahoma, and Austin for good. Derrick and me have worked out our own love grudge also. Derrick got to feeling so bad about me spending a month in the jailhouse, he went and paid for me a lawyer. My new lawyer got the charge against me reduced to simple assault by promising Mona's lawyer that Derrick and me would pay Mona's doctor bills. Mona had no insurance. I was released on my own recognizance. And to top it all off, Derrick rented a room at the Driskill Hotel, ordered take-out tabouli—my favorite—and after making the setting romantic with a candle and flowers, got down on one knee and proposed. Doesn't every girl dream of that?

So now life is back on track again except for my classes—which is why I hope you can find it in your heart to give me the W—and of course Mona's spleen, which the doctors removed. Even my rainbow tattoo is about to be finished. As soon as I get done writing this, Derrick is taking me down to Southside Tattoo, where they will add on the pot of gold. I only hope you can help me out with the W so that everyone but Mona can come out of this better off than when they started. And even Mona is getting her doctor bills paid. The cast is due to come off her leg real soon.

Very truly yours,

Opal Rogers

P.S. It seems to me like, if King Gilgamesh had gone looking for love instead of trouble, no snake on earth could have kept him from getting his life back on track again with a fresh start, just like Daddy and Mamma and Derrick and me. The only thing you need to make life new is love.

Sparks Alight

Mi querida Rosamunda:

Again I write to you, *cariña mia*, as I have written so often across the years of yearning. But today, for the first time *después de los años de añoranza*, you will read what I am writing to you.

I do not ask that you forgive me for speaking Spanish. You asked me to speak English when I stood beside you this afternoon, at first tongue-tied like a teenager overwhelmed by his first taste of love; then speaking in a rush, the language of the Quixote and of the Conquistadors gushing like lifeblood from my heart. "Speak English," you said, and I acquiesced. But now, as I remember discovering you, at last, in your front yard, amid all the broken things you have so carefully and so beautifully restored, the *castellano* bubbles from my fingertips like a hot spring from a lake of liquid fire. As I sit writing this *epístola del corazón* by the light of the moon in my attic garret—my emotion recollected in tranquility, as the poet Wordsworth said, and shaped into the song of a common man—I see again your exquisite lips like a candy-apple heart and feel the pieces of my broken life reassembled, restored, made whole. I hear your windchimes, like the philosopher Plato's music of the spheres, bringing harmony to parts of myself that I was sure would never know peace again.

I do not ask that you forgive me for calling the police. I will offer no excuses. We both know the strange and tragic circumstances that have brought me back to you at last. But I do ask you to suspend your judgment for the length of this letter from the heart. Please hear me out; and having heard, decide for yourself and for me what the best thing is for both of us.

I do not ask that you forgive my declaration of love. The great truth of my life has been my yearning for you. For me, it was *amor a primera vista*, a case of love at first sight strong enough to endure for almost forty years. Some say that they do not believe in the power of love at first sight. My granddaughter, *Cacahuetita*, with her victim's-eye view of the world, is such a person. But you and I, *cariña mia*, have lived long enough to know better.

I remember the day I first saw you as though it were yesterday, although almost four decades have passed. The moment is burned into my heart like light burns an image onto a piece of film. I have lived my whole life looking backward at the photograph that was captured in my heart: your candy-apple lips and your perfect caramel skin and your eyes that are the brown of chocolate as it cools from liquid to solid.

It was a frosty Valentine's Day, 1963. Snow covered everything on Congress Avenue, and the few people out and about shivered in the layered bundles of their clothes. But as you pulled up to the traffic light at 5th Street and Congress Avenue, you had the top down on your candy-apple red 1963 Cadillac, and your shoulders were bare. I glimpsed, across the intersection, your heart-shaped lips and your caramel skin and your hair blown back, and it was as though my senses had been dazzled by a solar flare. The molecules of air between us blazed like brilliant confetti that floats and dances, but does not fall—flashing sparks of gold that linked forever your perfect face and my love-singed heart. I felt the sparks alight on my skin like fiery pinpricks as your eyes met mine. In all the world there was only you and me, and the feeling of being one with the sparkling thing that the air had become. Then the traffic light changed, and you roared away with the wind in your hair. The fins on the back of your space-age Cadillac pierced my old-fashioned soul as you faded from view.

I wanted more than anything to chase you down, declare my eternal love, go down on my knees and propose. But I had just come from my wedding reception. My new bride—may God rest her soul—sat in the car by my side. We were on our way at that very moment to Corpus Christi for our honeymoon. So I let you go, *cariña mia*, even though my heart was exploding in my chest like a dying star. I wept like a child. And to my abiding shame, I told my new wife that my tears of unutterable grief at losing the love of my life were really tears of joy for our wedding day.

I have treasured that image of you, and of that moment, in my heart for almost forty years. And even though I was never unfaithful to my wife in the flesh, I have spent my life writing epistles of love to my vision of you. To you, *querida* Rosamunda, and to your heart-shaped lips, I have written thousands of letters and poems of undying desire.

When my granddaughter called me earlier today, and said that she had found my stolen rocking chair in the yard of her mother's killer—of the killer's grandmother, she corrected herself—I was sure that she had been driven to distraction by grief. How could I have known that she had found the love of my life?

When I pulled up in front of your house, after picking up *Cacahuetita* at the Stop N Go on Oltorf and South First—she was indeed beside herself, and the only way to calm her was to call the police—I saw the swooping fins of your 1963 Cadillac poking out of the open garage, and I felt my heart pierced again. But this time, the twinge I felt was one of pure joy. I had not given up hope, you see. My letters from the heart have been a lifelong cry of hope and love and light in a world that is all too often hopeless and loveless and lightless. But the police had been called already.

When we got out of my car and stood next to the rocking chair in whose headrest I carved Heaven for my dear departed wife, *Cacahuetita* was all for revenge. She spoke of seeing you handcuffed, taken downtown, forced to reveal the whereabouts of your grandson—may God have mercy on him. But the whole time I was silent, feeling hope sprouting like a rare flower from the dried-out husk of my life, and I asked my granddaughter to hold off judgment until the facts were known.

Then you came out into the yard, and I was struck deaf and dumb and blind to everything except your exquisite lips, and the third finger of your left hand. You walked over, in your grace and your beauty, and we all stood around the chair in silence. Only the windchimes spoke, dangling from the eaves of your roof and whispering in honeyed tones about the possibility of perfect harmony. Like me, they had seen that you wore no wedding ring. You had stained the rocking chair dark red, the color of blood that flows back to the heart to be burned bright red again—set afire with air from the lungs.

"I don't deal in stolen goods," you said, over the sound of the chimes. But you might as well have said, "*Te amo, mi querida.*" Because *I love you, my darling* were the only words I heard.

Cacahuetita began to speak harshly about her mother's murder. Then she spoke of vengeance. "An eye for an eye," she said.

But I waved her off, and gestured for you to speak your piece.

You said that your grandson had brought you the rocking chair, and that you had refurbished it as a way to try and make amends.

I said, "*Te amo, mi querida. Eres mas linda que nunca.*"

Cacahuetita thought that I had lost my wits, that I was talking to the chair; and she said so.

But the look in your eyes, *querida* Rosamunda, told me that you knew better. You knew that I had lost my heart again, like that moment almost forty years ago at the intersection of 5th Street and Congress Avenue. I know you saw me, too, on that day, *cariña mia*. Did the air blaze like brilliant confetti for you as well?

It was then that you said I should speak English.

So I said again, "I love you, my darling. You are more beautiful than ever."

Your melted-chocolate eyes said that you understood. But before you could reply, the police pulled up behind us, and things became even more confused than *Cacahuetita*'s lust for revenge. The police officers began to take statements; *Cacahuetita*'s first, then mine. Then they took the rocking chair, and you.

Just before you were escorted away, we exchanged names; you placed into my hands—hands sweating like those of a teenager looking into the eyes of his first love—the gift of windchimes; then you asked for the date of my birth in return.

I answered, "August 7, 1936."

As I write to you now, by the light of the gibbous moon through my open window and to the music of the spheres from your chimes, I wish I had answered that I was born on the day I first saw you. I have hung your chimes outside my attic window, and their song of love makes me pray with all my heart that I will see you again. The poet Wordsworth said that all poetry comes as the result of a transcendent moment, an instance of the sublime. You and I have shared such a moment. Every *epístola del corazón* that I have ever written has been a poem of love to you.

And so I ask you again, *querida* Rosamunda—I know that you have been released, because I called to check on your well-being even before I hung up your windchimes—to decide for us both what to do. For the first time in my life, my heart and my head speak as one. They say, "*Te amo, cariña mia.*" They say that I was not the only one who felt the burning sparks of love alight on that frozen Valentine's Day in 1963.

I ask you not to worry about the hearts of others. My granddaughter, and your grandson, will come to understand in time.

I ask for the chance to kneel at your feet and propose; and afterward, to make each new day in your life more beautiful than the last.

I await your answer.

Tu fiel Harry

Like Jacob and Esau

If you're looking for a Biblical allusion, Annie, you're sitting on the right stool. I'm talking Old Testament, one of the great brother stories of all time—except that the brothers in my version aren't blood relations; they're my ex-roommate, Pete, and me. I remember Rachel saying once that with Biblical allusions, the relationships are symbolical by nature. I guess Rachel would've known. Besides being one of God's chosen people, she was named after one of the key players in the Bible story I'm alluding to.

No, not one of the brothers, Annie! Am I living with a heathen?

Well, Rachel was named after a beautiful and faithful wife. How many patriarchs have you ever heard of named *Rachel*? I tell you what I'll do. If you can hang a nancy name on a single patriarch—we're talking Old Testament fathers now, real fire and brimstone men—your next two rounds are on me.

Hey, while we're on the subject, who's thirsty? Hey! Down at the end there! You thirsty? Just FYI, sir, *tipping* is not just something you do to cows. Thank you, sir. Thank you very much.

All right, Annie. To drink free or not to drink free—as a great *bard*-tender once said—that is the question. Take your best shot.

Aaron my ass. Do you know whose middle name that is? It's a good thing for you that this is Austin and not Memphis, Annie. You don't get free beer at my bar for calling the King a queen, even if you are the love of my life. Aaron isn't one of the brothers in the allusion anyway—although I guess it was his brother, Moses, who wrote the story down. My brothers aren't like Aaron and Moses at all. They're more like Jacob and Esau.

Yeah, you can call me Esau, Annie. That's the part I play, and I guess I looked it even then. Big-boned, redheaded, kind of hairy. But a real man's man, you know? My ex-roommate, Pete, plays Jacob. Pete fit the bill. Pale, kind of stringy, the hair on his chin so blonde and thin he almost never had to shave. Pete was a real mama's boy; but smart, and a talented musician to boot.

Rachel? Well, I guess she plays the part of herself— except that in my version of the story, it's Esau Rachel is interested in. Anyway, at first it's Esau. Then things get a little unhinged.

Moses's version of the story starts out with the Creation and works up from there. Mine begins with destruction instead—a burning apartment building and the death by fire of my best friend, Ben. You've heard that one before. My version begins with sleet hissing into an inferno and the north wind whipping the flames a hundred feet into the air. My version begins with me looking into that fiery furnace and knowing Ben was still inside. I remember the warmth of Pete's arm around my shoulders, even through my icy shirt, as we sat in the drainage ditch and watched the apartment building burn. I remember how the feel of that arm was like security, or sanity, or both; and how it made almost bearable the fact that we'd started the fire that took Ben. I remember thinking at that moment: *Pete is the brother I never had.*

So we settled in, in the absence of Ben, like the brothers we'd become—bound by a filial tie of fire. Pete and I spent even more time together afterwards than the three of us had before Ben burned alive. We rented a house with a fenced backyard and a laid-back pet policy. Pete rescued a charcoal-colored mutt from an animal shelter. I saved a kitten the color of ash. We all got domestic in a brotherly sort of way. Pete and I still competed together; still partied together; and most importantly, still dated together. Pete introduced me to Rachel, the woman I thought would be the one and only love of my life.

What changed my mind, Annie? The day you and Crockett moved in with me, of course, and taught me the real meaning of both *love* and *life.*

But back to the story. A lot like in the Old Testament, where Jacob met his beautiful and faithful Rachel one day at the well, I met a beautiful girl. In the modern version, though, it's Esau meeting Rachel; and the well is really a bar. We won't talk about the faithful part. At least, not yet.

Pete and I were down at the Crown and Anchor, kind of strung out from all the product we'd been sampling that night—more about that later—drinking pitchers of Guinness to balance our buzz and throwing darts to keep our minds off our minds, you know? Anyhow, up walks this flock of girls. There must have been eight or ten of them, I guess; but my whole world was focused on one. And to my great surprise, she was focused on me. She had short black hair and skin so pale you could see through it, but what took my breath away were her eyes. Her eyes were a color I'd never seen before, and haven't since—a one-time-only mix of green and brown and deep gold like looking into a river flowing slow over limestone in the late afternoon.

"Doubles?" she asked.

My tongue had gone as thick, all of a sudden, as the muscles of her swimmer's thighs. I had the feeling that my lungs were full of water. I ached for a pale-skinned, river-water-eyed lifeguard to cover my mouth with hers and fill my lungs with life-giving air.

"You know, darts?" she asked. "When you finish this game, would you like to play doubles?"

I had just gone down for the third time when Pete turned from throwing his last dart. "Bull's-eye!" I heard him yell. Then, "Rachel?"

Then he and my riverwater-eyed lifeguard were hugging like lovers reunited after a separation of years. After that came introductions. But I don't remember them much. I already had the only name I was interested in—that, and the fact that Rachel and Pete were only old friends.

I headed off to *unseal the well*—as Moses put

it—and by the time I got back from the bar with more pitchers of Guinness, my tongue had shrunk to its normal size. Rachel out-threw me at darts, which she played barefoot in a short red dress. She out-shot me at pool, which she also played barefoot, and that short red dress did interesting things when she bent over her cue. She out-drank me at the beer pitchers that Pete and I took turns keeping coming. In short, she swept me off my feet.

What was that, Annie?

Well, it might not have been Old Testament, exactly, all that womanly assertiveness. But *matriarchal?* No way. And later—much later, after many pitchers of beer—the male side and the female side kind of evened out. Leveled out, that is, back at Pete's and my place, side by side on the couch.

"You and Pete talk exactly alike," Rachel said, in a soft and sexy voice.

"We went through a life-changing experience together," I said.

"What does that mean?"

"Come here."

In the words of Genesis—and almost as much as you, Annie—*Rachel was beautiful and well favored.* And like Jacob of old, I would have worked seven years, and yet seven years again, to have her.

Except that I'm Esau, remember. And work I did. It wasn't hard work, so much as work that was hard on me. You see, Pete and I had started our own business. Coke, X, crystal, pot—if you wanted it, we could get it. Cash on the barrelhead, Annie. Parks and pot; hackey-sack and mushrooms; lakes and crystal; clubs and ecstasy, and always cocaine. And all that money, money, money. Hundred-dollar-a-chip backgammon games, and twenty-dollar-ante poker. We even went to Cancun, Pete and me and Rachel and Rachel's blonde friend named Jenny. Beaches and booze; monuments and mushrooms; parasailing and pot; clubs and ecstasy, and always cocaine.

Those were great times for Rachel and me. But with

all that product always lying around, and all that cash always coming in, things with Pete got a little sketchy. I started losing somehow, every time we played. Not so much at backgammon, but always at cards. And cards was what Pete always wanted to play—five-dollar-a-point gin was his favorite game—until all the money that was coming in seemed to be flowing straight to Pete.

Then came the night I finally caught Pete cheating at cards. We were playing gin–and snorting cocaine, of course–and when Pete bent over to do a line, through the smoky glass of our kitchen table, I saw a wad of cards underneath his leg. I yanked him up, and cards and coke and drug paraphernalia went flying. When I slammed him up against the wall, the lying sack of shit swore it was the first time he'd ever cheated; and then he begged me not to hit him in the face.

There were tears in his eyes, Annie.

All I could think about was his arm, warm around my shoulders there in that frozen rain, as the flames swallowed Ben. And I couldn't even punch Pete in the gut. What I did instead was throw him out of the house, which put a stop to the gambling and the drug business, not to mention the much-beleaguered atmosphere of brotherly love. But we were still bound by a filial tie of fire—and by ties of another kind that I had yet to discover.

I spent a lot of time afterwards asking myself what could've happened. What was there, in all of Creation, crooked enough to twist what could've been into what was?

I have a picture of Rachel and me together in that house Pete and I shared—messy but not filthy, strewn with old newspapers and drug paraphernalia and assorted sporting goods. In the picture, Rachel and I are sitting on the couch and smiling. It is a beautiful black leather couch, bought with drug money. Rachel and I are nestled against each other like two people who have spent every free moment, waking and unwaking, tangled in each other's arms. She is wearing that short red dress from our first night together. I am wearing a purple-and-green-patterned Guatemalan shirt that sets off my red hair. Rachel's face, pale beneath her black hair, lightly touches my own. She holds up the kitten I rescued from the animal shelter all those months ago—a fat, ash-gray fur-ball, almost full-grown. In better times, Pete and I had named him Ben. But there is no sign of Pete in the picture.

Yes, of course, Annie. He was holding the camera.

Now the allusion takes a strange turn, and my version and the Bible story go their separate ways. The way Moses tells the story, Jacob has two wives. In my version, Rachel has two husbands. Not literal husbands, of course. But like Rachel said, with Biblical allusions, the relationships are symbolical by nature. Like I told you before, when Pete moved out, Rachel moved in with me.

Of course we weren't legally married, Annie. Just living together, like I said. But I thought the rules would be the same.

Well, like I said before, Pete and I kept seeing each other. I even let him keep his charcoal-colored mutt in Rachel's and my backyard. I guess I hoped that maybe my keeping the dog would go a little way toward making things right between us. I should've known when Pete's dog kept trying to screw my cat that nothing would ever be right again. But the dog also ate one of Rachel's favorite shoes. So it seemed like maybe just the dog, you know?

Then things started to go wrong with Rachel and me. We didn't sit as close as before; and unlike the days when we first started seeing each other, when Rachel and I would double-date with Pete and one of Rachel's flock of swimmer friends, Rachel wouldn't hang around Pete and me at the same time anymore. She was never at the house when he came by. And those riverwater eyes I'd spent so many months staring into wouldn't even look back into mine. I was desperate enough to tell Pete what had been going on, and ask what he thought about it

"Give her some time," Pete said. "Tread water for a while."

But it was like trying to swim ashore in a riptide, Annie.

Finally, I asked her straight out. I sat her down on the couch, that same expensive black leather sofa purchased with ill-gotten gains of Pete's and mine. I kissed the pale skin on her cheek ever so gently. And then, in a voice every bit as gentle as my lips on her skin, I asked what was going on.

"Pete and I," she said, heaving a breathy swimmer's sigh, "have been seeing each other."

"And?" I asked, nodding encouragement. Of course she and Pete had been seeing each other. Pete's dog lived in our backyard.

"We've been sleeping together."

"Sleeping?" I asked. It still hadn't hit me. You see, in addition to being a trusting soul by nature, I was in love.

"Slept together," she said. Her riverwater eyes, for the first time in what seemed like months, looked deep into mine. I saw tears in them. "We slept together. Once. Twice. Three times maybe."

"Three . . . "

"But it was only one night."

"Oof," I choked out. I felt as though my lungs were filling with water. "Where?"

"Right here on the couch," she said, the tears and the story flowing freely now, together, "while you were asleep in the other room. But it didn't mean anything. We were both so messed up, I hardly even remember."

I sat there not breathing. Drowned.

"Things can be all right again between us, can't they?" she asked, after a while. "Well, can't they? At least say something."

I had a picture in my mind of the two of them on the couch together—her with that red dress riding up around her hips and Pete lean and pale and naked, with that thin blonde hair on his chin. "It's all right," I said, finally. "It's going to be all right. I have to leave for a little while. Can you find someplace else to stay, just for to-night?"

"Where are you going?"

"The liquor store."

When Pete came to visit his dog, later that day, I was sitting out on the side porch drinking whiskey. It was a beautiful fall day, the sky clear-blue and empty. The north wind gusted with just the least edge of a chill. Pete came walking up from the side, the way he always came up. He liked to park his convertible Mustang—a cherry red '65 model with a white leather interior bought back during the days when our business was booming—next to the side porch so he could keep an eye on it through the sliding glass door. I took a long pull, grinned, and handed him the bottle.

Pete was never a man to turn down a drink. We wound up sitting there the whole afternoon, drinking booze, slapping each other on the back, pretending we were brothers again—the same way Pete had when he cheated me at cards and slept with Rachel behind my back. But today Pete wasn't the only one pretending.

Yeah, Annie. Unlike in the Old Testament version of the story, this time it was Esau wearing the disguise. It wasn't an animal skin, exactly. And I didn't bring a savory meat dish. What I brought instead was a lying-sack-of-shit personality and a couple of bottles of Jim Beam.

"So what's the occasion?" Pete asked after a while.

"Nothing much," I said, almost casually. "I just split up with Rachel."

"Yeah?"

"Yeah," I said, managing a grin. "I want to celebrate being single again."

"Single, huh?" Pete asked. "Well, you're better off is what I say. I never liked old Rachel much anyway."

I grinned and nodded, shaking with rage. Pete sat a little in front of me, in a wooden rocking chair. I sat on the concrete floor with my back against the wall. Behind me, within easy reach, sat the tire iron I'd taken from the trunk of Rachel's car.

Pete and I each held a bottle now, and I clinked mine against his just a little too hard. "To brotherhood," I said, and reached for the tire iron.

"Brotherhood?" Pete asked. "You sound like Ben."

At the mention of Ben's name, I took my hand off the tire iron. "Do you remember the day Ben died?" I asked, fighting to keep my voice steady. "When we sat there in that drainage ditch, caked with ice but with our arms around each other, and watched the apartment building burn?"

"Sure," Pete said. "I remember. It was awful."

"Not for me," I said. "At least, not completely. I mean, what happened to Ben was awful. But I felt that day like you were the brother I never had."

"Yeah, me too."

"Yeah? And do you remember the day I told you that Rachel and I were having problems?" I asked, reaching again for the tire iron. "You told me that I should tread water, remember? But you—"

"Ah, hold on a minute there, brother," Pete said. "I gotta whiz." Then he bolted inside.

Strange as it may sound, the urgency of that bladder pressure probably saved Pete's life. That, and my whiskey buzz. By the time I fumbled the tire iron out from behind my back and made it into the living room, Pete had ducked into the bathroom and locked the door. As I stood there next to the couch, thinking about Pete and Rachel tangled up together—their sweat-dampened skin pale against black leather—I guess I must've wigged out a little. When I was finished, there wasn't much left of the sofa. And all that rage I'd so carefully built up had flashed and faded away. By the time Pete came back from the bathroom, I just felt numb.

"What the hell happened to the couch?" Pete asked. His face had gone dead white and his hands were shaking.

"What does it look like?"

"Like it's been ripped to shreds," he said. "There's

stuffing all over the house." He waved an arm at the shredded couch, the stuffing-covered living room.

"I wanted it to be you," I said, and held up the tire iron. "But you were in the bathroom. Wanna use this on me?"

"On you?"

"Yeah," I said, handing it over. "Do me a favor, brother. Bash out my brains."

"I'm not your brother," Pete said. He held the tire iron limp-wristed and looked at me like I'd lost my mind. "Are you insane?"

"Oh, we're brothers all right. Just like Jacob and Esau in the Bible. But the relationship is symbolical."

"Symbolical my ass," he said. "Jacob and Esau don't kill each other. At the end of the Bible story, Jacob gives Esau gifts, then they kiss and reconcile." He handed back the tire iron. "Take this gift."

Pete was right about the Bible story. But I swung the tire iron hard against his cheek anyway. "Take this kiss," I said.

What can I say, Annie? In an allusion, anything can be symbolical. Even a reconciliation kiss.

Waltz the Milky Way

I am the Prophet Mudcat. I am the one who tastes the secret desires of all others.

Come and taste them, too.

Think of the trendone as a catalyst. No, as incentive. No, as a stimulus package for the human condition, crafted to jumpstart the sexual economy of humankind. Think of the trendone as the cantilever of a cable-stayed span connecting each individual to the collective unconscious.

Think of the trendone as the heart of a love bridge.

In the coming age of love, the harsh isolation of day will give way to cool darkness as the composite depths of the human ocean are plumbed. In the coming age of love, you will never be alone.

Consider this. Hot young stars bathe in a cauldron of gas at the heart of the Milky Way Galaxy, stars packed so tightly together that the stellar wind of each collides with the winds of all others to form a halo thick as liquid at sixty million degrees. Think of each star as a human body and each wind as a pheromone current. Think of life as a blazing water ballet. Think of white-hot bodies twisting, tasting, whirling, waltzing—bodies all afire and yet unconsumed.

Come and waltz the Milky Way.

I felt a gentle shaking; and startling awake into the crusty feel of dirty kitchen clothes and the lingering stink of duck-gut gumbo, I recognized the here-and-now of Manager Joe's office corner and the Sexless Redhead kneeling beside me. For the first time in my life I felt relieved to wake up fully clothed, and afraid I was about to be sliced up into catfish gumbo, at the same time.

The Sexless Redhead said: Wake up, Bo! Drag your lazy ass up off that laundry pile and come with me.

I said: Thanks. But unless you're planning to cook and eat me, I'm comfy right here.

The Sexless Redhead flashed a close-lipped smile,

and shook his or her head at me.

She or he said: Gunshow, and a cup of joe.

I said: Excuse me?

He or she said: What you should've asked just now was who the hell was I, and where the hell was I wanting to take you. So that's what I answered.

I said: You want to take me to a gun show?

She or he said: Shake it off, Bo. Gunshow is what they call me around here. I'm headed up to the breakfast counter to get some coffee. Come on up and share a cup.

I said: Thanks again. But like I said before, I'm comfy right here.

Gunshow's close-lipped smile faded as fast as it had flashed.

He or she said: Don't be a jackass, Bo. The day manager will be here any minute. If she catches you asleep in this office, she'll put an end to your new dishwashing gig, lickety-split.

I said: But Manager Joe said—

Gunshow said: Manager Joe would've said anything to keep from washing them dishes himself. Now come on, or don't. It's all the same to me whether it's you in that dishpit tomorrow, or some other shit-out-of-luck son of a bitch. Truth be told, I don't even know why the hell I'm doing this.

To my surprise, I felt myself actually grinning up at Gunshow.

I said: Okay, I'll bite. Why the hell are you doing this?

She or he flashed that close-lipped smile again, and nodded down at me.

He or she said: Manager Joe swears you're out of your freaking mind. In my book, that means you must be all right.

She or he stood up then, and reached a hand down at me.

I reached up and took it. The skin on his or her palm felt as thick as the pad on a dog's paw. The grip was firm, but not painful, and possessed of a wiry strength that I felt pulsing through Gunshow's entire body as she or he lifted me up off the pile of clothes.

I said: Howdy, Gunshow. They call me Mudcat.

Gunshow said: I'm proud to know you. Now let's get that cup of . . . Jesus Christ! What's that on your face?

I said: I guess I am a little stubbly. But I didn't figure I needed a clean shave to work the dishpit.

She or he said: I ain't talking about whiskers. Leastways, not the kind I ever saw on a man before.

I said: What do you mean?

He or she said: It looks to me like you grew out a set of catfish feelers.

I said: Oh no.

I ran to the nearest bathroom and checked my look in the mirror. Gunshow followed me in, pointing to the pair of wormlike protuberances that must've sprouted over the course of my sleep and now occupied the corners of my mouth.

Gunshow said: Oh yes. Them are sure enough catfish feelers. Barbels, I believe they're called. I recognize them from my grabbling days back on the Washita.

I said: Your what days back where?

I was too busy looking at my face to engage my brain. The twin fleshy protuberances did indeed look like catfish feelers. And they weren't the only new additions to my facial anatomy. There seemed to be a good bit more to my nose than I remembered. I leaned closer to the mirror. Yes, my nose was definitely larger. It was shaped differently, too—broader at the base, more pronounced generally, and connected to the barbels at the corners of my mouth by thin lines of lip-colored flesh radiating diagonally from each nostril.

Gunshow said: Grabbling is a kind of fishing I used to do back in Oklahoma. Every spring the catfish nest in underwater caves and lay their eggs. Instead of using lines or nets to catch them, you wade into the water, stick your arms into holes in the banks, and yank yellow or white or flathead catfish out with your bare hands. I'll never forget the tickle of them catfish whiskers in that cold muddy water.

Just then, Gunshow reached up and tickled my left barbel with his or her index finger. I simultaneously tasted and smelled the duck-gut gumbo on Gunshow's finger, and felt an electric bite from the contact that made me jerk back. I felt Gunshow jerk back, too; and instinctively, I touched the barbel with the tip of my tongue. It was bizarre. At the same moment, I was tasting and feeling the barbel with my tongue, tasting and feeling and smelling my tongue with the barbel, and feeling—with both tongue and barbel—an electric jolt like you get when you touch both poles on a car battery. I yanked my tongue back into my mouth, still tasting the charge and smelling the ozone in the air.

I said: I've grown an electric earthworm mustache.

Gunshow said: Yep. Now I need you to get your catfish face out of the women's bathroom. There's a mirror in the men's, if you're not done looking at them barbels. Once I've freshened up a little, we can get that cup of joe.

I said: I think I need a breath of fresh air.

I walked slowly through the preproom and sat down on the steps out back, trying not to think about anything at all. The horizon was just starting to pale with the coming dawn; and through the live oak leaves overhead, I could see the last bright stars. I lay back on the steps and looked up, breathing deep. For a fleeting moment, I felt as though I could close my eyes and erase the insanity that my life had become—as though, when I opened my eyes again, the world would look and taste and feel the same as it had before my sea change. I breathed out slowly, trying to remember the view from the overpriced balcony of my undersized new condo. But what flashed across my mind instead was a familiar amphibian presence.

The salamanders said: We suppose you would like to whine about the new nose.

When I finally opened my eyes, I saw the stars shining through the oak leaves like a brilliant surprise—clearer and closer, and more familiar, than they had ever shone before. I knew the name and type of every bright light in the winedark sky; I knew which lights nurtured islands of intelligent species; I knew the name of each species, and the names of the things each produced and consumed. And I realized, with a glimpse of inner clarity rivaling even the most impressive feats of my hybrid eyes, that the gifts the salamanders had given me far outweighed the life I had lost.

I said: To tell you the truth, I kind of like the new nose. It's got character. The old nose was a little small for my face.

The salamanders said: Our feeling exactly. And you will find that the new nose is as functional as it is beautiful, equally efficient in the air and in the water. The modified mucous membranes, blood vessels, and bony structure of the new nose combine to warm and humidify air en route to the lungs, cool blood destined for the brain, control the flow of water, and filter out foreign particles. The resulting improvement in your sense of smell will aid in finding mates, detecting predators, and even evaluating the emotions of the chattering chimp-cousins that surround you.

I said: Like I said before, I like the nose. But I need you to get that electric earthworm mustache off of my face.

They said: Mustache?

I said: The disgusting barbels that run from my nose to the corners of my mouth.

They said: Disgusting? Why, your barbels are nothing short of debonair! After the new nose, they are your most distinguished feature.

I said: They're going to get me killed. You have to get rid of them.

They said: Impossible. Your sense of smell and touch in the water, as well as your ability to navigate in murky conditions, depends on those barbels.

I said: Then you're going to have to find some way to make them internal, or retractable, or some such thing. It's either that, or I'm cutting them off myself.

Just then, I heard the clomp of cowboy boots behind me. I sat up and turned to see Gunshow walking out onto the porch. It struck me suddenly, remembering how I'd been kicked out of the women's bathroom, that Gunshow must be female—at least, anatomically speaking.

She said: Hell, Mudcat! You don't need to cut off that earthworm mustache. What you need is to grow you a beard—a funky Fu Manchu!

The salamanders said: We quite agree! A Fu Manchu would compliment the new nose quite nicely, and cover the barbels as well. It would also go a long way toward establishing your credentials as the charter member of the Planet Earth chapter of the Intergalactic Society of the Cosmically Hip.

I said: I've never grown out what you'd call a real beard before. I'm a little worried that . . . well, that my facial hair might be too thin.

Gunshow said: The peach fuzz thing is your lookout. I got problems of my own. Now, come on. Let's get that cup of joe.

I looked at Gunshow again, with her thumbs jammed into her pockets and her boots sticking out over the edge of the porch, and I realized that the Prophet Mudcat had found his first friend. Then she clomped back into the preproom, leaving me alone.

I said: Gunshow? Wait!

The salamanders said: Go ahead. You need not worry about the barbels, or your previous inability to grow a beard. This is a scenario we are prepared to handle.

I got up and padded after Gunshow. Sure enough, as I made my way across the wooden porchboards and onto the concrete preproom floor, I felt a weird tingling in the lower part of my face. I reached up and touched my chin, running my fingers across the thick prickles I found there. I felt the prickles lengthening into bristles; felt the bristles sprouting into bushy hairs on my chin and around my lips; but—despite a half-panicked finger-search of other body areas—I didn't feel hair sprouting anyplace else. The salamanders had not only turned on my beard-growing function, they were shaping my Fu Manchu as they grew it out.

By the time I wound my way to the front of the restaurant, the tingling had stopped. I reached up, ran my fingers across my face again, and felt a sleek Fu Manchu where there had only been peach-fuzz stubble just minutes before.

I felt like a leper made clean by a Jesus miracle.

But as I walked up to the breakfast counter and found Gunshow sitting between a frowning, obviously confused Manager Joe and one of the most beautiful, saddest-looking women I had ever seen, it became clear that—as had been the case with so many of my previous miracles—there had been some kind of salamander glitch.

Manager Joe said: Gunshow! What the hell are you doing sitting down? We're in transition in the back of the house, and in the weeds on the waitfloor! The kitchen is freaking slammed! I need you to prep five trays of home-fries on the fly, and then get your ass on the line! While you're at it, go find Chay! She's supposed to stay on the waitfloor until the first day waiter clocks in. And you! Bluebeard! Who the hell are you?

I said: Mudcat. The new latenight dishwasher. Remember?

Manager Joe said: Dude, I didn't recognize you with that funky blue Fu Manchu.

I said: Did you say *blue*?

Manager Joe said: I said *funky blue Fu Manchu*. Hello? The ring of blue hair around your mouth that comes to point underneath your chin?

I said: My new Fu Manchu is blue?

I stuck my upper lip out as far as it would go and cut my eyes down toward it. But my beautiful new nose was blocking my view.

Manager Joe said: Do you by any chance recall the names of the drugs they gave you in that loony bin? Lithium? Was that one of them?

I said: I'm not schizophrenic. I'm just confused.

Gunshow said: It ain't just Mudcat that's confused, Manager Joe. The reason I'm sitting here drinking coffee is that I just finished a double shift. I clocked out half an hour ago. And the way I understand it, Mudcat was never on the clock at all. Now pour yourself a cup of coffee, Mudcat, and sit down here with Bonnie and me.

I said: Bonnie?

The beautiful, sad-looking woman turned her gold-flecked green eyes on me. I noticed her pale, clear skin; and noticed how, around her eyes, that perfect skin was red and swollen with crying. I noticed her slight aroma of lavender, mixed with the salty tang of tears. And with the aid of my hybrid senses, I realized that the woman sitting next to Gunshow was the most breathtaking and heart-broken creature I'd ever encountered.

The sad, lovely woman said: Bonnie Bailey. Hello, Mudcat. I like the funky new blue Fu Manchu.

I said: Really? Or are you just saying that to keep from hurting my feelings?

Bonnie said: No, I love it. If I were a man, I'd want one just like it.

Gunshow said: Me, too. And I'd want to grow it out just as fast.

Bonnie said: Excuse me?

I said: Nothing. Enough about me. Let's talk about you. Would you mind if I asked you a personal question?

Bonnie said: That depends on the question.

I said: What on earth could make so lovely a creature look so sad?

Bonnie said: Kurt.

I heard her voice quaver as she said it. Then I saw and smelled the bitter tears that started to well out of her gold-flecked green eyes. I would've given anything on earth for a handkerchief to dry them. But I had nothing, not even shoes.

I said: Who, or what, is a Kurt?

Manager Joe said: Kurt is late, of course! Kurt is the reason we're in the weeds on the waitfloor! Kurt is on the verge of being unemployed . . .

I said: I was talking to—

Manager Joe said: I wasn't finished! I know two other people who are about to become unemployed, if they don't hop their asses up, pronto, and start helping!

I saw Gunshow hop up, saw Manager Joe start around the counter toward me, and saw the sad and lovely Bonnie wipe her eyes with the back of her hand.

Bonnie said: Kurt may be all of those things. But he's also the only boyfriend I've ever had.

Still lacking a handkerchief, but feeling as though I had to do something—anything, and quickly—to make Bonnie feel better, I remembered the vial of trendone that was stuck down into my Speedo. And in the momentary confusion, I slipped a trendone mickey into Bonnie's coffee cup and pushed it toward her.

I said: Here, take a drink of this. It'll make you feel better.

Bonnie took a long, slow sip. Then another. And another. Then she sniffled a little, and looked up at me with those sad, lovely eyes.

She said: Thank you, Mudcat.

I said: Go, and cry no more.

Then Manager Joe was pulling me toward the kitchen, talking a mile a minute about opening duties that I had no clue how to perform. I slipped the trendone vial back into my Speedo; and by the time I looked back, the sad and lovely Bonnie had vanished from the breakfast counter.

Manager Joe said: Dude! This really is your lucky day. Less than twenty-four hours after training to work the dishpit, you're about to train to work the hoststand. How about that? From the back of the house to the front of the house in less than a day.

I said: That dishpit shift was about as much luck as I can handle in a less-than-twenty-four hour period. And besides, I'm barefoot. Isn't there some kind of law against serving food and drinks without shoes?

Gunshow, who was trying to squeeze past us in the throughway, stopped dead in her tracks and squared her shoulders at Manager Joe.

She said: Law or no law, didn't I hear Manager Joe promise you a pair of boots and socks for that dish shift? Where the hell are they? And while we're at it, where's your tipout? I saw them latenight waitfolks giving Manager Joe money to give to you.

I said: Tipout?

Manager Joe said: Gunshow, I thought I told you to prep homefries. What are you doing standing here in the waitstation?

Gunshow said: I prepped the homefries before I clocked out. I was on my way to look for Chay, and to clock back in again, before I hit the kitchen. But before I do, I want to see Mudcat get what's owed him. Or I swear to God, we'll both walk out of here and leave your crooked ass to fend for itself.

Manager Joe reached into his pocket, pulled out a wad of damp one-dollar bills, and stuffed them into my hands.

He said: Okay, okay. Here's the tipout money. I was just holding it for you. I'll head out to the storage room and see what I can do about boots just as soon as I've taken orders on the waitfloor. In the meantime, make fresh tea and coffee. Okay?

I said: No way. I'm not working another shift for nothing. And we both know I can't clock in.

Manager Joe said: Jesus. What do you want now?

I said: I need a place to sleep for the foreseeable future. And Gunshow says that sleeping in the office will get me fired.

Manager Joe looked from the waitfloor, which was

filling up with even more morning patrons, to the kitchen, which was still unmanned. Then he looked at me.

He said: There's a cot in the storage shed that I use sometimes to take naps between shifts. You can sleep there for as long as you need to. For that, plus tipouts, plus boots and socks, plus clean clothes, you work the dishpit and the hoststand, and do whatever else I tell you to—and I better not ever have to tell you to do anything twice again.

I said: You've got yourself a dishwasher and a host trainee, Manager Joe.

Manager Joe said: It's about time. Gunshow, help Mudcat get tea and coffee made, and the waitfloor set up. Mudcat, get your ass in gear.

Gunshow said: I thought you wanted me to work the kitchen. I can't do that, look for Chay, and train Mudcat at the same time.

Manager Joe said: Alright, alright. Just focus on the kitchen. You can yell directions at Mudcat while you're throwing down breakfast orders. Now move!

I counted and faced the fourteen damp one-dollar bills that Manager Joe had just given me, and slipped them into the pocket of the pants I'd earned the night before. Then, to the shouted directions of Gunshow, I started brewing an urn of regular iced tea and an urn of hippie tea—a funky-smelling, reddish-pink-colored, herbal concoction that could be served iced or hot—and also started brewing three pots of coffee. Almost faster than seemed possible, Manager Joe was back in the waitstation hanging tickets and shouting drink orders at me.

Manager Joe said: Whip me up sixteen Aqua Vitae Blends and four large O.J.'s on the fly. I'll be right back with footwear.

I said: What's Aqua Vitae?

But Manager Joe had already disappeared into the back of the house.

I said: Gunshow! What's Aqua Vitae?

She said: Hell, where I come from, Aqua Vitae is

white lightning. But it can be almost anything that's potent and distilled. In Kentucky it'd be whiskey, and brandy in France. It just depends on where you happen to be when you're doing the brewing. Here at the Aqua Vitae Café, it's our own special blend of coffee. The place is named for it. But you'll have to wait until it quits brewing before you can pour it out for Manager Joe. What you should do right now is run creamers to the waitfloor.

So while coffee and tea were brewing, I ran creamer setups to every table on the waitfloor, fielding more orders for coffee and orange juice from the growing crowd that was filtering in. I looked for Bonnie as I made my slow way from table to table, but there was no sign of her. Finally, I slipped a trendone mickey to every customer in the restaurant by dividing the remaining contents of the vial into the tea urns and the coffee pots. Then I poured out the sixteen Aqua Vitae Blends and four large O.J.'s that Manager Joe had ordered, plus the six Aqua Vitae Blends, two hippie teas, and three small O.J's that I'd taken orders for myself. In the kitchen behind me, I heard the sizzle of pancake batter on the griddle as Gunshow worked to fill the orders Manager Joe had hung in the window.

I said: Where has the sad and lovely Bonnie gone?

Gunshow said: To look for the lousy and unfaithful Kurt. She came by to bring him a clean apron for his hostshift, but he wasn't here. I imagine he's out back banging Chay—it wouldn't be the first time.

I said: Kurt fools around on Bonnie? Why on earth would he do that?

Gunshow said: Why on earth would a man do anything?

Just then, Manager Joe burst around the preproom corner and handed me the boots and socks that he'd promised. The boots were not new. But they looked to be in good shape, and the socks smelled freshly-washed. While Manager Joe trayed up the coffees and O.J.'s I'd brewed and poured, I tried on my new footwear. To my complete surprise, both the boots and the socks were a perfect fit. I walked a tight but comfy circle around the waitstation, then headed for the men's bathroom to check the look of my new beard at last, noticing on the way how the steel-toed business ends of my new boots were roomy enough to accommodate my newly-webbed toes.

Back in the bathroom, though, my entire world focused down onto my funky new Fu Manchu. The Fu Manchu was indeed very thick and very nicely shaped. It was also very, very blue.

I said: Salamanders, you bastards. Why blue?

The salamanders said: To be perfectly honest, we are not quite sure why the new Fu Manchu is blue. The whole notion of body hair—facial or otherwise—is frankly revolting to our species. But what a rare and delightful color! Do you have a term for it?

I looked closer at the Fu Manchu.

I said: I'm not quite sure what to call this color. It's deeper than sky blue, but lighter than aquamarine. If I had to make a guess, I suppose I would call the shade of my funky new Fu Manchu—

My speculation was cut off as a big dark-haired guy in an Aqua Vitae t-shirt burst into the bathroom. He bent over the sink, squirted a double handful of soap from the dispenser, and frantically started scrubbing his face and hands. Then he looked up at me, squinting hard at my new Fu Manchu through the suds.

He said: Robin's egg.

I said: What the hell?

He said: The color of your beard. It's robin's egg blue.

I said: No. I meant, what the hell is that smell?

My newly-enhanced olfactory senses had detected a strange and powerful odor. It seemed to be coming from the stranger who was bathing in the sink. Despite the hospital smell of the soap he continued to slather onto himself, my hybrid senses were overwhelmed by the hot combination of perfume, cigarette smoke, and female pheromones—a cocktail of aromas that there was no mistaking as the reek of fresh sex. I noticed that the stranger had rinsed the soap off himself now, and started scrubbing his apron. Then I felt a stirring that made me suddenly, and very awkwardly, aware of the trendone vial stuffed into my Speedo.

The stirring in my Speedo was immediately followed by the return of the salamanders.

The salamanders said: Robin's egg blue? How quaint, and how curiously appropriate! On another note, judging by the contents of your bathing suit, it would appear that—like your new nose and your new barbels— the third key element of your love prophet anatomy is functioning perfectly.

Before I had a chance to answer, there came a pounding on the bathroom door, followed by the screams of a megalomaniac manager in a rush.

Manager Joe said: Get your asses out of that bathroom right now! Kurt! Mudcat! Let's go!

It struck me that this dark-haired stranger must be the boyfriend who was making the lovely Bonnie so sad— with the smell coming off of him and his apron, there could be no doubt that Gunshow had been right about him being unfaithful.

Just then, Kurt set the water in the sink to gushing; and as he rinsed the soap out of his apron, he started talking rapid-fire.

He said: Your name is Mudcat? Are you new? Can you hand me a couple of towels?

I said: Yes, yes, and yes.

I handed Kurt a handful of paper towels; then I watched as he turned off the water and started patting himself, and his apron, dry.

Kurt said: Did you happen to see a hot blonde come in earlier?

I said: Yes.

Kurt said: Details would be a plus. Did she look pissed? Was she carrying an apron? She was supposed to be bringing me a clean one. I bummed this one off Chay, one of the latenight waitresses. But I think it's too funky to wear.

Just as Kurt finished speaking, Manager Joe threw open the door.

Manager Joe said: You won't be needing an apron, Kurt. You're fired. There's a write-up form on my desk that you may remember, since you signed it the last time you were late. It was your final warning. Basically what it says is that the next time you're late, you're unemployed.

Kurt said: Harsh.

Manager Joe said: But fair. You're going to have to leave the premises.

I said: Could the two of you please leave the bathroom? I've got a little business to take care of.

Manager Joe said: Five minutes. Then get back to work.

I bolted the door behind them. Then I looked at my reflection in the mirror again, still smelling the hot sex aroma and thinking of what the Salamanders had said about my love prophet anatomy. I took in the new Fu Manchu. It was indeed robin's egg blue, and it perfectly covered the barbels. I took in the new nose. It was indeed larger, more prominent; in the words of the Salamanders, it was *debonair*. Finally, I compared the size of the trendone vial in my Speedo—a standard test tube that I'd lifted from the water treatment plant—to the size of the stirring that had been caused by the hot pheromone scent. And I saw, with a sinking feeling, that they were the same.

Then I was struck with a flash of inspiration truly worthy of the Prophet of Love.

I said: Salamanders!

The salamanders said: Yes?

I said: The new nose is great. The new barbels are great, in combination with the new Fu Manchu. But I'd like to talk to you about another enhancement.

They said: What sort of enhancement did you have in mind?

I said: Well, maybe *augmentation* would be a better term.

They said: To what?

I said: To my . . . What did you call it? Oh yes . . . the third key element of my Love Prophet anatomy.

They said: We understand. This is another scenario we are prepared to handle. But remember, Prophet Mudcat, to whom much is given, much will be required . . .

So I sing you this siren song, my soon-to-be brothers and sisters, as I start my new daily routine. I work the dishpit and the hoststand at Aqua Vitae Café. I lie in the sun on the carpet grass lawn beside Barton Springs pool. I glean trendone in the gloaming from beneath bright red salamander tails.

Then I return to Aqua Vitae Café, to deposit the fruits of my evening's harvest into the tea urns and coffee pots. In my new capacity as host, one of my duties is to serve my potent distillation to the customers I seat. Brothers and sisters, you have only to relax and enjoy!

Come and drink with me.

Tahini Is a Sesame Seed Paste

This is important.

Remember—Tahini is not the name of an actual assistant professor in the Arts and Humanities Department at River City Community College. Tahini is a sesame seed paste.

For the record: At faculty meetings, people with Ph.D.'s do not shove tape recorders into each other's faces and snarl, "Say that again for the record! Say that again for the record!"

For the record: No charges of harassment, counter-charges of discrimination, or counter-countercharges of reverse discrimination have been filed at the highest levels. The ACLU is not involved.

For the record: There is no Reign of Terror mentality. No soon-to-be ex-colleagues glare sideways at each other in the hallways with a mix of bloodlust and fear.

This is very important.

Remember—Tahini is not, at this very moment, running roughshod over the Arts and Humanities Department at RCCC with a posse of ACLU lawyers at his back. Tahini is a key ingredient in hummus, the traditional Middle Eastern chickpea spread.

For the record: I have no proof that Tahini is either a stalker or a harasser.

Off the record: Tahini preys on female students, part-time instructors, and newly-arrived colleagues who don't know the score.

Off the record: I have it on good authority that Dr. Dido, the lovely redheaded adjunct who overdosed on Zanex, was involved with Tahini. I spoke with Dr. Dido about Tahini just before her breakdown; and as she stood and stared without blinking, all she could say was, "He makes me feel like a victim."

Off the record: I feel like a victim myself.

148

*   *   *

It is important to keep in mind the fact that I have a wife and son to support.

Remember—Tahini is not in league with the forces of darkness. Dr. Dido is not the name of an ex-part-time instructor in the Arts and Humanities Department at RCCC. Tahini, sometimes called sesame butter, is often used in Middle Eastern sauces and eaten on chicken and fish. Dido, a legendary queen of Carthage, kills herself for love of a foreign adventurer in Virgil's *Aeneid*.

Off the record, I am not the only one to speculate that Tahini is in fact a terrorist—the thin end of an al Qaeda wedge being driven into American Arts and Humanities Departments—seeking to wreak havoc on the Western canon by causing conflict and confusion, and suing for discrimination when called on the carpet for his crimes.

Off the record: If Tahini was a coyote on my old man's ranch, and I was my old man, I would perforate Tahini's hide with a high-powered rifle and hang it up to dry on a strand of barbed wire.

For the record:

Dear Dr. Omega:

I am writing to make an informal complaint about aggressive and insulting conduct on the part of Tahini and to ask you to intervene.

As I told you in our meeting yesterday, Tahini has been harassing me for some time. Since we first met in the Summer of 2000, almost every time Tahini and I have come into contact, he has engaged in name-calling and insulting behavior. While the names I have been called are not obscene, and many of the insults are juvenile, they are all mean-spirited and meant to wound. This is a pattern behavior on Tahini's part. This pattern behavior constitutes harassment. And this harassment has got to stop.

I have on multiple occasions told Tahini that his actions are unacceptable and his comments unwelcome, and asked him to be civil when speaking to me. He has consistently disregarded my requests. The most recent incident occurred yesterday (Thursday, November 15, 2001) in the Arts and Humanities office. I simply said "hello" to Tahini, and he proceeded to insult me and call me names. I informed him again, pointedly—and in front of witnesses—that his harassment was unacceptable. I warned him that if he insulted me again, I would be forced to take formal, written action against him. When he got up from the computer to leave the room, he insulted me again.

Tahini delights in causing pain—not only for myself, but for others in the department. Dr. Dido was one of them. I am therefore filing this informal written complaint and asking you to take action. Thanks in advance for your prompt attention to this matter.

Sincerely,

Joseph Jasmine, Ph.D.

For the record: This is the actual letter I submitted to Dr. Omega.

For the record: Dr. Omega made no attempt whatsoever to influence the filing of my complaint.

Off the record: I used my own letterhead for the complaint letter, and changed the word *formal* to *informal*, at Dr. Omega's request. Dr. Omega said that using official departmental letterhead to file a formal complaint against Tahini, especially in the aftermath of September 11th, would too greatly restrict his range of response options as Dean of Arts and Humanities at RCCC.

Off the record: If I was my old man, I would have punched Dr. Omega in the face.

It is important to keep in mind the fact that I had to take a second job to make my house payment.

Remember—Tahini is not a chain-smoking, desert-spawned demon. Dr. Alpha Omega is not the actual name of the current Dean of Arts and Humanities at RCCC. Tahini, made from ground sesame seeds (sometimes baked first, sometimes not), is used in Middle Eastern cooking to flavor such dishes as hummus and baba ghanoush. Alpha and omega are the first and last letters of the Greek alphabet.

Off the record: The names Tahini has called me under his foul cigarette breath include *Dr. Joey, Joey Boy, Little Joey, Dr. Hayseed,* and *Dr. Cowpie.* He continually asks me which barnyard animal is the best in bed.

For the record: I have no proof that Tahini has shared either the nicknames or the bestiality question with any of my students.

Off the record: If Tahini didn't, who did?

It is important to keep in mind the fact that I owe more than $43,000 in student loans.

Remember—although my old man's name is indeed Joseph Jasmine, and he did cosign my mortgage note, he lives 162 miles southwest of here on a cattle ranch. The real Joseph Jasmine is not connected in any way with the informal complaint against Tahini that his son filed on personal letterhead with the Dean of Arts and Humanities at RCCC. My old man was not the one Dr. Omega intimidated by talking pointedly, in the dry heat of his office, about the repercussions of filing an unfounded official complaint against Tahini, in the current post-9/11 climate, on departmental letterhead.

Off the record: The first time my old man saw that my personal letterhead said *Joseph Jasmine, Ph.D.* instead of *Joseph Jasmine, Jr., Ph.D.,* he looked like he'd just cracked the ice off the water troughs on a blue norther morning and had two hundred cattle yet to feed. "I ain't buried yet," my old man said. "And I ain't no doctor."

Off the record: My response to my old man was that both *Jr.* and *Ph.D.* would be too much of a mouthful; and that as an assistant professor in the Arts and Humanities Department at RCCC, only *Ph.D.* was important.

Off the record: My old man wouldn't look me in the eye for a long time after that.

Off the record: If my old man knew I'd changed *formal* to *informal* in that complaint letter, he would never look me in the eye again.

No Good in Goodbye

You give your life to a man, and all he gives you are lies. I look at Kurt standing beside me in the moonlight. Then I look away into the moon. I can see the man in it. Low, almost full, the moon straddles the hills west of Austin as though the man in it is bending down for an open-mouthed kiss.

"I know," I say.

"You know what?" Kurt asks, and smiles at me. His smile is a beautiful lie.

"I know about your new girlfriend," I say. I feel the concrete-and-steel retaining wall of the First Street Bridge cool against my fingertips, and feel Kurt's breath warm against my cheek. But my eyes are on the mouth of the man in the moon.

"Are you kidding?" Kurt asks.

We met on the bus in middle school. *KT + BB = LOVE FOREVER* was the message Kurt carved into the soft metal wall of that old Bluebird not long afterwards, next to the seat where we first kissed. I've lived my life by those words ever since. He is the only man I have ever loved, his lips the only lips to have warmed the most secret parts of my body. But Kurt's lips have warmed the secret places of so many others.

"I need you to be honest with me," I say, giving him one last chance to save our life together.

"You're looking at the sole honest man in Austin," he says.

I roll up onto my tiptoes and stretch my lips toward the mouth of the man in the moon. He seems so close now—so low over the hills and Town Lake and the statue of Stevie Ray Vaughn at Auditorium Shores—that I should be able to reach up and touch his open mouth with mine. I lean out over the wall, stretch my lips into the air, and feel nothing. The man in the moon is just another cold and lovely moonlight lie.

153

"I know about you and Chay," I say. I take a long look back at Kurt as I climb up onto the wall. They are laughing now, those lips that have been saying *love forever* since middle school—the luscious, lying lips of the self-proclaimed *sole honest man in Austin*. The man I wanted so much to believe, so many times, that I've been living blind. "Everybody knows."

I close my eyes, strip the dress over my head, and toss it back into a past I will never look at again. There is no good in goodbye.

When I leap off the First Street Bridge, my eyes are open. I strike the surface of the lake with a thunderclap that flashes through me and then fades to distant flickers. I do not feel myself floating. Instead, I feel as though I am hovering in the air. I see my body below me as it glides face-down in the water, carried by some miracle of current upstream.

I feel neither current nor breeze. But I see the moonlit water washing the lies from my skin as I make my slow way across Town Lake. In the Bible, when Abraham went to save Sodom and Gomorrah, he went looking for ten honest men. Just one would be enough for me—and my eyes are wide open.

In the moonlight, the halo of my hair makes me look like some kind of water angel as I glide open-eyed across the surface of the lake to the feet of the statue of Stevie Ray Vaughn. I am still me, still Bonnie. But at the same time I am an angel, searching the depths of Town Lake, and along the shoreline, for one honest man in Austin.

But the man in the moon is a lie told to little girls who ride Bluebird buses.

The man I left behind on the First Street Bridge will flee the city like Lot fled his cities of sin.

And Stevie Ray Vaughn is long gone, a pillar of salt, quicksilver as the moon reflected in the surface I'm floating on, and above. He is looking back. I am looking forward into a place where lake and shore and sky become one.

I do not feel my lungs fill with water.

Second Sight

All along the waterline of Livingston, Guatemala, where the Golfete empties Lake Izabal into the Caribbean Sea, there are brightly-painted wooden houses with boats pulled up in front like battered lowriders in South Austin driveways. The town consists of a main street lined with hip, high-dollar, eco-tourist restaurants and hotels, and two cross-streets lined with restaurants and hotels that are cheaper and funkier.

With my daypack on my shoulder, my rucksack at my feet, and a sixteen-pound hangover-hammer banging inside my head, I stand at the front desk of the cheapest and funkiest hotel in Livingston, waiting to return my room key. Through the open door to my left, I can see the first of the three bars where I blew all my quetzales last night—listening to reggae from the islands, taste-testing every brand of rum until there were no more brands left to taste-test, and talking to this wild Irish girl who claimed to be the queen of the elves.

In all the rum-bleared haze of last night, what stands out is meeting Mab.

Mab had a thing for Lynyrd Skynyrd. Her favorite song was "Mr. Breeze." Every time the reggae stopped, she'd climb up onto a table and belt out, "Call me the breeze, I keep blowin' down the road," in a drunken Dublin brogue. Obnoxious, but none of my business; at least it wasn't "Freebird." I guess we would've gone the whole evening without speaking to each other—Mab stumbling on and off of the tabletops, sticking her tongue into the mouth of every eco-tourist in the place; me sitting alone on my barstool, mumbling into my rum—but when she stumbled up onto the bar and kicked over my shot-glass, I told her that Mr. Breeze was about to meet Mr. Boot.

"I'm Queen Mab," she said, "you very rude Yank. I don't suppose you know who Queen Mab is."

"Mab is an Irish witch," I remember saying. "Isn't

156

she?"

"You're not as drunk as you look." She stepped down out of the beer lights and sat next to me in the red neon humidity of the bar. "In myth, Mab is the Queen of Connacht, the combined mother-warrior aspect of the Triple Goddess. In literature, Mab is the queen of the elves. In the flesh, Mab is an Irish drinker and dancer and lover. How about you, Mr. Boot?"

"Call me Kurt," I said.

"All right, then. How about you, Kurt?"

"In myth, Kurt is a drinker from Texas, a rum-taster of epic distinction. At least, that's what the literature says."

"Brilliant! My dancer over there isn't a drinker." She pressed her forehead against mine—hers was wet from dancing—and stared straight through me with eyes that were gold-flecked green. "So much for myth and literature. What about Kurt of the flesh?"

"Kurt of the flesh plans to taste-test rum until he's blind, then feel his way back to the hotel."

I proceeded to do just that.

Anyway, I suppose that I did. It occurs to me, as I hand my key to the desk clerk and collect the ten-quetzal note I had to leave as a deposit for the key, that the last thing I clearly remember are Mab's parting words: "When we meet again, it'll be fiery; and you'll buy me a drink."

To my surprise, I see Mab again at the little comedor I stop into for a spicy hangover-soaker—fiery chicken pepian with hot chiles, tomatillos, tomatoes, and squash seeds—and enough steaming coffee to wake the dead. She sweeps in, plunks her rucksack down next to my table, and takes my coffee cup.

"Hello again, darling," she says, as I start to protest. "Didn't I tell you that you'd buy me a drink the next time we met?"

"I am forced to admit that you did."

"Second sight, darling," she says. Then she proceeds to tell me how she was robbed at machete-point by the dancing partner I left her with—a big lanky Garífuna with dreads who called himself Jon B. He took her on a moonlit walk into the jungle, she says, and stopped next to a beautiful flowering tree; then he pulled out the machete he must've hidden there, and told her to hand over her cash. She wasn't hurt and hadn't lost much, just what quetzales she had left after a long night of drinking and dancing. "Luck of the Irish," she says, all hot Gaelic blush and breathless. "To go for a walk in the jungle with a dancer who doesn't drink, and is more interested in armed robbery than in putting his arms around me. I should've known to stick with the drunkard."

"If drunk is lucky, I'm your man," I say, studying Mab. She doesn't even look shaken up. As she sits there drinking my coffee, Mab looks excited. Aroused. Her cheeks are flushed; and her breath, between sentences, comes in shallow gasps.

"It looks like Mab's luck has finally turned for the better." She finishes my coffee and moves on to what's left of my soup, asking between bites where I'm off to with my daypack on the table and my rucksack at my feet.

"Honduras. Bay Islands. And you?"

"Call me the breeze," she says. "I keep blowin' down the road."

"More Lynyrd Skynyrd?" I ask, half-smiling. "Have you forgotten what I told you last night at the bar about Mr. Breeze meeting Mr. Boot?"

"Relax," she says, "darling boot. It looks like the winds of fortune are finally blowing your way."

After a stop at the bank, we take a fast fiberglass launch to Puerto Barrios, Guatemala, for fifteen quetzales apiece. Puerto Barrios is one of those medium-sized towns so common down here defined not by sight or sound, but by smell—sewer and smoke and exhaust and garbage. From there we catch a bus to Finca la Inca, where I've been told we can go by motorboat to the Honduran border at El Limite, and then by canoe through the swamp to the Honduran entry post at Cayumelito.

On the way to Finca la Inca, our packed third-class bus lumbers stop-and-start through miles and miles of banana plantations that belong to The Standard Fruit Company. Banana fields stretch as far as the eye can see. US Army-type outbuildings, rounded and ribbed in the style of World War II, appear from time to time among the banana trees, intermixed with clustered clapboard shacks. Everyone on the crowded bus smells like Puerto Barrios. Myself. Mab. The other passengers—mostly short, leather-skinned plantation workers who get off and on at the shacks lining the caliche road.

"Wage slaves," Mab says. "Not a one of them makes more than a dollar a day."

"Jesus."

"Not Jesus," Mab says. "Uncle Sam. You Yanks have been bad boys."

"Some worse than others," I say.

Mab pierces my blue eyes with hers that are gold-flecked green. "Is that why you're here then, darling? Because you've been a bad boy?"

"You mean, here on this bus?"

"I mean here in backwoods Guatemala," she says. "You Yanks don't often get down this way. The only other two Yanks I've met were bad boys indeed. Drug runners with a boatload of cocaine. *Fruit of the coca bush*, they called it. Fun boys, they were. But very, very bad."

"Well, this bad boy is here to sample the fruit of the sugar cane." I pull a silver flask full of last night's rum from my daypack and tilt it back. "And by the way, never call a Texan a *Yank*."

Mab grins at me, all bright red Gaelic hair and bad teeth, and takes the flask. "One of the functions of the mythical Queen Mab was to confirm the new-crowned king," she says gravely. "I hereby confirm thee King Boot, frontier drinker and lover." Then she tilts back the flask and returns it to me.

"I decline the confirmation," I say, splashing rum onto my fingers and touching my forehead, "and anoint myself Kurt the Fool."

"A fool for love?" Mab asks.

"Not any more."

"Darling," she says, "you're forgetting that Queen Mab has the gift of second sight."

"This is the second time you've made that claim," I say. "Are you seriously trying to tell me that you have the power to see the future?"

"But of course. The power to pierce the veil of time with my mind's eye, darling, and peer into what lurks on the far side. The past, present, and future are but counties in the kingdom of the Faerie Queen, and all women of Irish descent are her ladies in waiting."

Our third-class bus is a big rickety Bluebird, not air-conditioned. Except for the blue-and-white Guatemalan flag paint job and the bells and whistles of folk music blasting over the loudspeakers, it could be the same Bluebird bus I used to ride to Lamar Middle School, back when the world was a bright blue possibility that was bound to turn out well. It occurs to me that Mab and I are sitting in the same seat—third from the back on the left-hand side—that I always shared with the only real girlfriend I ever had, Bonnie Bailey, another pale-skinned beauty of the Irish persuasion with gold-flecked eyes like Mab's. I carved Bonnie's and my initials, along with a sappy middle-school message of love, into the soft metal wall of our Bluebird during the last hot gasp of an Indian summer.

I share all this with Mab, along with the fact that Bonnie and I stayed together all through middle school, high school, and after. Then we spend some time looking for my initials and Bonnie's, along with the sappy message I carved: *KT + BB = LOVE FOREVER*. We find a lot of carved messages—*Trabajar es morir*; *Es mejor reir que maldecir*; *Yankee go home*—but nothing that has anything to do with first and only real love, or sweaty first kisses stolen from Bonnie Bailey in the early-September heat, or the hot wet feel of Mab's leg pressed against mine.

The conductor calls out the Finca la Inca stop, and Mab and I wade through the boxes and bundles and bodies of passengers pressed tight in the aisle, and stumble off the bus. The conductor climbs up into the rack on top, throws our rucksacks down to me, then swings back inside as the Bluebird lumbers away in a cloud of black smoke. We stand there, Mab and me and the flask we're passing, in the diesel-smelling air that is even thicker and more humid, somehow, than the air on the bus—air so thick and wet it feels like breathing water.

We look around for Finca la Inca, but there seems to be no Finca la Inca here to see; just a muddy embankment in front of us and the rush of fast-flowing water on the far side. Behind us, the banana trees stretch away to the jungle that lurks at the edge of things visible like a recurring bad dream.

"It looks like my karmic chickens have come home to roost," I say.

"What a fey thing to say," Mab says. "What does it mean?"

"Just that I've been a pretty bad boy, even for a Texan. And there seems to be no Finca la Inca in sight."

Mab grins and hands me the flask. "Fortify thyself with a draught of this, Sir Fool, and screw your courage to the sticking-place. Then we'll see what karmic chickens lurk on the far side of yon mound of mud."

We charge over the embankment together—stumbling, belly-laughing, rucksacks bouncing—and down the muddy slope to the edge of a river in flood. There are three big dugout canoes pulled high on the bank. Each canoe looks to have been carved out of a single, huge tree; and all three have outboard motors mounted on their sterns. There is a little open-air shack not far from the canoes. Three men and a pregnant woman stand underneath it. When we walk up, the woman listens while the three men talk to us about Jesus, and about us all being brothers in Christ.

"*Somos todos hermanos en Cristo,*" they say and

grin. Their teeth are worse than Mab's.

"*Hermanos y hermanas*," I say.

"Brothers and sisters," they say, "but of course."

Then they shaft us out of forty quetzales apiece for the ten-minute boatride to El Limite. They let us off at a house in the middle of the rainforest, alongside a canal that winds away into a swamp, and tell us to go with God.

"*Vaya con Dios*," they say. "*Vamos a encontrarnos en el otro lado.*" We will meet again on the other side.

As Mab and I walk into the yard, I catch sight of a fenced-off set of buildings on the far side of the house with a weather-beaten sign out front: *MINISTERIO DE RELACIONES EXTRANJERAS*. But whether the foreign relations are Honduran or Guatemalan is anybody's guess. From the dilapidated look of the buildings, the post has been closed a long time. The rainforest that surrounds the buildings, and us, is a shade of green I've never seen before—almost the color of a carpet grass lawn in Austin, but a million times more intense. Here at the edge of the swamp, the air feels even wetter, and the stink of rotten vegetation is thick. Mud is everywhere, dark gray and slimy. It sticks to the bottom of our hiking boots as we cross the yard.

A woman sitting on stacked crates on a covered porch tells us that we must wait for the boat to come back from taking some Cokes downriver. There are crates of Fanta Orange and Coca-Cola and a beer called Salva Vida, and the woman asks if we'd like something to drink.

Mab and I have a cool Salva Vida each, and talk a little with the woman, who is probably forty but looks sixty, her skin the same leather as the wage slaves of Standard Fruit. It turns out the woman is a wife, with a grown daughter and two small kids who come out onto the porch while we're talking. They all live, along with the woman's husband, in the little house that doubles as a combination grocery and liquor store. The wife refills my flask with rum for five quetzales, then tells me flat-out that I can't drink it here. "*No debes bebirlo aquí.*" Her husband, a government official, cannot allow liquor to be drunk on the premises. "He is out on patrol now," she goes on to say in that no-nonsense Spanish, "but he is due back at any moment."

The man of the house comes riding up on a horse just as we are finishing our Salva Vidas. He is dressed like a civilian, but carries a pistol in a military-style holster on his belt. The horse, a bay stallion, looks poor. Maybe even a little sick. I can count his ribs, and he keeps trying to forage in the bare mud. When I reach up to scratch him between the ears, I find that his mane is filled with ticks.

It occurs to me only after the fact that I must've made a face when I felt the ticks. The man on the horse, who had been neutral up until that moment as he studied Mab and me, suddenly puts a hand on the butt of his pistol and gives me a look that makes it clear he's about to use it. He says in Spanish, rapid-fire, that the Central Americans are the slaves of the North Americans. Then he spits on my boot.

I don't know what to say, so I say nothing.

A light rain starts to fall, and the quiet draws out into the sound of water dripping from leaves. It occurs to me that I am going to die here in the rain at the edge of this swamp in backwoods Guatemala, with a glob of spit on my boot. It occurs to me, strangely, that I am not afraid. Instead, a feeling of what I can only call relief runs through me, as cool as the rain on my face. I remember what the three men in the dugout said about meeting again on the other side, and for the first time since I saw Bonnie Bailey strip off her dress and leap naked—pale skin flashing white in the moonlight—off the First Street Bridge in Austin, my heart feels almost free.

"*¡Los centroamericanos son esclavos de los nort-americanos!*" the man on the horse says again and pulls the pistol from his holster. "*¡Contesta!*" he says.

But I have no answer to give. I look quietly up at the revolver pointing down at me, cool relief running through my heart so strong now that it seems to have stopped the stream of time—past, present, and future. In the past, Bonnie Bailey hangs in the moonlight with her arms spread like wings, and the scent of her skin on the dress she tossed down to me lingers in the air like the last words she spoke before she leapt out into space: "I know about her . . . Everybody knows." The present is the stink of rotting vegetation and the sound of water dripping from leaves. The future is a finger on a trigger and a hammer clicking back. Mab is silent. The wife and grown daughter and the two kids on the porch are silent. I find myself wondering whether they feel relieved, too.

Then the silence is broken by the sound of a motor, followed by the sound of a boat cutting through water, and the canoe we've been waiting for grinds onto the bank—back from delivering its load of Cokes downriver. I feel the stream of time start to flow again, but the past is all I see. I see Bonnie Bailey disappear beneath the First Street Bridge, and I find myself counting slowly. When I get to four, I hear her smack the surface of the water a hundred feet down.

"I'm sorry," I say, at last. "I'm sorry for everything."

"It's not his fault," Mab says.

"It is his fault," the man on the horse says. "His, and others like him."

"Yes," I say. "It is my fault. And I'm sorry for it all."

The man on the horse looks at me as if this isn't the answer he expected. The expression on the face behind the revolver is half-questioning, half-disbelieving—as though I'd just popped out of fairyland and told him I was confirming him king. Then there comes the sound of another motor, followed by the sound of another canoe cutting through the current, and one of the big dugouts from Finca la Inca grinds onto the bank with three more back-packers aboard. The man on the horse looks at the backpackers, then at me. Then he holsters his pistol, yanks the horse's head around, and rides off into the jungle, back the way he came.

"That was the bravest thing I've ever seen," Mab

says, after a long moment. I feel her arms wrap around me and squeeze me tight from behind.

I shrug myself free, yank the flask out of my day-pack, and tilt it back. The no-nonsense wife, despite her warning earlier against drinking rum on the premises, doesn't say a word.

Twenty quetzales apiece buys us all a canoe ride through a swamp worthy of the name, overgrown with trees and filled with cattails and brush and wild bananas. We slice down a channel that is, at times, narrow enough for the boat to scrape the grass on either side, and at other times, wide enough for us to swing around trees at reckless speeds. We bounce off half-submerged logs, leaning hard to the left and right in order to make the tight bends in the channel. Big green hills loom ahead in the mist. Egrets and cormorants explode out of the water and swoosh over the boat at irregular intervals, and we see a small herd of Brahmin cattle stranded on an island.

We scrape underneath a barbed wire fence, finally—ducking down into the bottom of the canoe—and pull up at a bare spot on the grassy shore that has been worn smooth by the docking of boats like ours. We unload our gear and walk about a mile along a path through mixed jungle and pastureland to a tiny hamlet called Cayumelito. It is starting to rain again and the light is fading, turning the jungle into a vast dripping shadow that is not quite green, not quite black. I'd been told that we could stay the night in Cayumelito, but there is no hotel. There are no buses or cars even, just a few empty shacks and a tightly-built little hut that must be the border post. And in the fast-falling dark, the border post is closed. The jungle around us has gone black, and it comes to me that we are stuck; and here in the blackdark country between Guatemala and Honduras at night, where there are no police or soldiers, there is no law.

The three other backpackers start walking again, talking among themselves and sounding as nervous as I feel. They are headed toward a town called Tegucigalpita, an hour away on foot, where they say there is a bus that runs to San Pedro Sula, Honduras. It only takes a moment for them to vanish, the fading sound of their voices tracing their progress down a dirt road into the jungle night.

Then, to my complete surprise, Mab slides her arms around me and presses her mouth against mine. As if the surprise weren't complete enough, I feel her slip a hand inside my shorts. Her breath tastes of rum, and her hand feels cold and wet as she takes hold of me and starts to work me up.

"What can I do?" she asks. "What can I do to please you?"

"You can't," I say. "Come on. We've got to go."

"C'mon yourself, King Boot," she says, working me harder. "Your queen is in need."

"Mab," I say, taking hold of the arm connected to the hand in my shorts, "if we don't catch up with the others, we'll be stuck here all night. In the jungle. Alone."

"Luck of the Irish, darling. Danger is an aphro-disiac for Queen Mab."

"I'm leaving," I say. "With or without you."

This seems to get Mab's attention. We gather up our rucks; and after Mab changes her hiking boots for shoes, we start walking quickly through the steady rain. I can tell from the sound of their voices getting closer that Mab and I are gaining on the other backpackers. Then Mab's pace starts to flag. I hear the sound of voices start to fade into the darkness ahead.

"Mab," I say, "let's move!"

"Darling," she says, "relax! The Faerie Queen has a premonition that the winds of fortune are about to blow our way."

I'm about to tell her where she can put that pre-monition when I hear the sound of an engine behind us; and less than a minute later, a truck with Texas plates pulls up and stops. Then the man inside cracks his win-dow and asks if we want a ride.

"Poof!" Mab says. "What did I tell you, darling?

Second sight."

After a little negotiation, and five quetzales apiece, we climb up into the back and start through the blackdark country—Mab and me, and the other three backpackers who came running back to us when they saw the truck. We all get off in the central plaza of Tegucigalpita, then Mab and I negotiate some more with the driver through the crack in the window.

The truck driver is from Honduras, he says. Only the truck is from Texas. He says he'll take us to San Pedro Sula for eighty lempiras apiece—lempiras are dollars, Honduran-style—which he says is a bargain fit for a king. We talk him down to eighty total, then tell him there's a problem. We've only got quetzales and U.S. dollars.

"Having dollars is never a problem," he says. "Climb aboard."

We drive through the rain over rough roads, going over some bridges and around others, fording rain-swollen creeks in the dark, until we get to Puerto Cortes. There we stop at a little restaurant—a covered patio with tables, sticking off the side of a stucco house—and eat a very late dinner. At the table, we don't talk much. Mab and I are soaking wet, and about half-drunk and half-hungover. The truck driver, who calls himself Pepe, keeps looking at Mab as though he can see through her shirt. He says that if we change into dry clothes, we can ride in the front with him. I pay for the meal in dollars and get change in lempiras, which makes the restaurant owner very happy. He says that we can change clothes in his house, if we do it quickly.

So Mab and I change together, in the same little bathroom. Her skin is pale, her breasts full, with cold-hardened nipples. In the small of her back, she has a butterfly tattoo that is silver and black and midnight blue, so delicate it seems almost alive. Except for the tattoo, Mab's body reminds me so much of Bonnie Bailey's body—so pale and smooth, with breasts that bloomed from buds to D-cups as the down on my face slowly

167

hardened to scruff—that I have to squeeze my eyes tight-shut and dress in a self-imposed dark that is as bleak as the country we are traveling. Mab reaches for me, as I knew she would from the time we walked into the little bathroom together and started to take off our clothes.

"Don't," I say. "Please don't." The churning in my belly feels exactly the same as the moment I looked over the retaining wall of the First Street Bridge, and saw Bonnie's naked body floating face-down in the moonlit water with her arms spread wide.

"C'mon lover," Mab says. "It's now or never."

"Never," I say. "Never again."

Then Pepe is knocking on the door, saying that it's time to take off for San Pedro Sula. So we finish dressing quickly, Mab and me, then heave our rucksacks up into the back of the truck and climb into the cab.

From the moment the truck starts moving, things are tense. Pepe tells us that he's an auto salesman in San Pedro Sula, and that he's delivering this truck that he bought in Laredo to his used car lot. *"Compré el camion,"* he says again and again—I bought the truck—which makes me absolutely sure that it's stolen. Then he pulls out a silver box and spoon kit, and asks if we'd like to do some cocaine.

"Darling," Mab says, "I thought you'd never ask."

I say nothing at all. But when Mab tries to pass the box and spoon to me, after taking a hit for herself, I shake my head.

Mab sniffs, smiles, takes another one to grow on, and passes the kit back to Pepe.

Then I see Pepe put a hand on Mab's leg. He just rests his hand on her inner thigh at first. But soon he starts to rub her leg, slowly working his hand higher and higher, until it disappears inside her shorts. Mab smiles a close-lipped smile, slides forward a little, and puts her hand on Pepe's thigh. Then she reaches over and rubs a hand on my thigh as well—giving me a third chance, apparently. When she slides her hand inside my shorts this time, I feel myself start to come to life.

But just then the engine cuts out, and we coast to a stop about halfway between Puerto Cortes and San Pedro Sula. I lean out of the truck—feeling Mab's hand inside my shorts and seeing again Bonnie's naked body floating on the surface of Town Lake—and throw up every bit of the food that I ate in Puerto Cortes. When I raise my head, I see that by some miracle, there is a service station not far up the road. I tell this to Pepe, who has been too busy with Mab to look up. He gives Mab another spoonful from the silver box, then says that the two of them should go and find a mechanic together.

"Fat chance, lover," Mab says. "It's raining out there."

You must go, he says. "*Tienes que ir.*" Then he says that no mechanic in Honduras would fail to come to the aid of a girl who looks like Mab.

"You're going to leave me," Mab says. And as Pepe climbs out of the truck, she pierces me again with her eyes that are gold-flecked green. "You're going to abandon me here."

"No," I say. "This time you're wrong. After all, where would I go?"

Mab says nothing. She just climbs out after Pepe, and the two of them head off up the road side-by-side, leaving me standing alone next to the broken-down truck.

Then, poof! A bus pulls up, bound for San Pedro Sula. Second sight, Mab would say, if she were here. I look up the road after her, but she has disappeared inside the service station with Pepe and his box and spoon.

"*¿Estás veniendo?*" the conductor calls out. Are you coming?

I remember seeing Mab with one hand on Pepe's thigh and one hand in my shorts. I remember feeling myself start to stir for the first time since I last saw Bonnie Bailey naked and alive—her skin faerie-pale in the moonlight—telling me she knew about the other girl I'd been seeing. I remember watching Bonnie floating away from me on the surface of the lake that was as silver and black and midnight blue as a butterfly tattoo . . . and wondering how she knew.

"*¿Estás veniendo o no?*" the conductor calls out again.

I haul my rucksack from the bed of the truck and climb onto the bus, thinking again of the butterfly tattoo in the small of Mab's back. It is only that part of her I am thinking of as I pay my three-lempira fare and we pull away, leaving Mab alone with Pepe in the blackdark country.

Danger is an aphrodisiac, Mab said once. I wonder if she is saying it now. In my mind's eye I see Pepe's hands gripping the small of Mab's back, covering those wings of silver and black and midnight blue—the only difference between Mab's body and the body of Bonnie Bailey—and I realize that Mab's tattoo is not a butterfly at all.

It's the Faerie Queen.

Music of the Spheres

We all seek perfect harmony to release us from this cycle of rebirth. I have spent my life in pursuit of the synchronization of heavenly bodies, and the reflection of this heavenly perfection in our imperfect bodies here below. Our lives are reflections only—shadows cast by lights that swing and dance above us all, pulling us along in the blindness of our earthly days and ways.

So I sit down, Harry, after reading your letter, to chart the pattern of the planetary dance. As I listen to the windchimes ringing beneath my eaves, I know many things even before I begin. I know that you have hung the chimes I gave you. I knew even before you wrote to me. I have heard them ringing all evening—a shadowy reflection of the music playing outside my screen door—in harmony with my own.

I place a white cardboard square on my round kitchen table. Across the top of the far edge I write in red letters: *Harry: August 7, 1936*. Then I write in blue letters: *Rosamond: July 9, 1938*. Underneath our names and birthdates I draw a circle within a circle, both black. I split the circles with six black lines. I place the twelve houses in their positions. I place the ten planets—the eight non-earthly planetary bodies plus the Sun and Moon—into the houses in which they were located when you and I were last born again into this world of sorrows, drawing the planetary symbols in bright green.

I seek to make connections, Harry—drawing the trines and squares connecting your planets in red, the trines and squares connecting my own planets in blue. I watch the red and blue lines crossing and re-crossing, the triangles and squares of our destinies coming together inside the twin circles like a beautiful spider web in which you and I have been trapped since our last rebirths. I seek to know whether each of us can complete the other, whether we can help each other escape this earthly cycle and begin to dance at last among the lights of heaven,

171

swinging together forever to the never-ending music of the spheres.

I sit in my kitchen, burn sage in a silver bowl, and listen to the sound of your windchimes and mine. When I tire of charting the positions of ten heavenly dancers at two moments more than sixty years distant in time, I pause, breathe deeply of the burnt-sage scent, and write down the things that I already know. I use a number two pencil on a yellow legal pad.

Rosamond: Cancer. Cancer is the fourth sign of the zodiac and its symbol is the Crab. Positive Expression: for Cancerians, family obligations are paramount. We are the most nurturing and protective of all signs—sympathetic, softhearted, deeply feeling and nurturing. We possess gifts of imagination, intuition, and insight. We tend to develop mutually dependent ties with people we care about, and expect to be looked after in return. Negative Expression: hypersensitivity and indulging in self-pity. Since we are emotional, touchy, and easily hurt, we learn to master our turbulent moods by being secretive and suspicious. Cancerians are good at developing psychological defenses when it comes to avoiding confrontation; but when we attack, we would rather lose a claw than release our prey.

Yes, Harry, this is me. Both the positive and the negative are me. Like everyone else in this earthly circle, doomed to live and die and live again, I am a two-sided coin. I have the possibility to turn for good or for evil. My husband—may God have mercy on his soul—always said that I was his good luck. *Buena suerte*, he always called me, and on the day he won the Cadillac convertible—drawing to an inside straight after I touched his cards—he was right. My son, and my grandson after him, called me *bruja* and made the sign of the cross behind my back. May they both come back as cockroaches in a bad cook's kitchen.

Harry: Leo. Leo is the fifth sign of the zodiac and its symbol is the Lion. Positive Expression: Leos belong in the center of their world—confident and self-assured, capable of managing and leading, becoming influential and prestigious. They are warm, affectionate, funloving, and optimistic. They radiate confidence. Negative Expression: Leos hate taking second place and always try to lead whether they are capable or not. The Leonine shadow can be overbearing, dictatorial, and narcissistic. Leos love to show off and adore being center stage.

Yes, this is you, Harry. I knew you were a Leo before you told me the date of your birth. I knew it when I walked out of my house and saw you standing there with your beautiful flowing beard and your long white braid and your head in the clouds. Only a lion could carry his head that way. But I could tell, by the way your granddaughter's eyes went timid when you spoke, that you have been a tyrant to her.

I finish our chart at last, but before I look at our composite planets, I make a strong *yerbabuena* tea and sweeten it with honey. I take out your letter and read it again. Then I sit at the table, take three slow sips of *yerbabuena* tea, and begin the reading. I interpret the groupings of green planets in black houses. I gauge the complementarity of the red and blue trines and squares within the black double-circle. I write down the connections and their connotations. I use a number two pencil on a yellow legal pad.

Sun in the Seventh House: Sun in the Seventh House of the composite chart is an excellent position for an equal partnership. The Seventh House is the house of partners. So this is the best position for a marriage or a joint business venture. It denotes a complementarity that makes the whole stronger than the parts. One warning: the Seventh House is not only the house of partners, it is also the house of open enmities and intimate conflict. If

173

*our relationship is not going well, we may compete with
each other in a way that is disruptive and produces
antagonism.*

It is a good beginning, Harry. It is an evil beginning
as well. I shared the Sun in the Seventh House with
Arturo, and for us the coin spun toward conflict more
than partnership almost from the beginning. But Arturo
was crazy—crazy for me, and crazy for gambling. He won
the Cadillac convertible, but lost our life savings. He begot
a crazy son on me, who begot in his turn a son who was
crazy, and who took the life of your daughter-in-law. The
Bible speaks of the sins of fathers. It should speak of their
insanity instead.

*Sun Conjunct Mars: composite Sun conjunct composite
Mars is a combination filled with energy. This relationship will arouse strong forces in us that can be used for
getting a great deal of work done or for making changes
in ourselves. We will have many discussions. This relationship can grow through creative conflict. But if we
suppress our anger and instead express it indirectly, the
relationship could turn into an endless stream of argu-
ments. Since Sun conjunct Mars is an indication of physical vitality, we should take part in vigorous physical
activity together whenever possible.*

I shared this connection with Arturo as well, Harry.
But the only physical activity Arturo was interested in
resulted in the begetting of his crazy son. Mars rules the
sex drive. Perhaps we could take up walking to balance
out the other activity. But there is much of Arturo in you,
Harry. I saw it in your lovely leonine eyes.

*Sun Conjunct Pluto: the conjunction of composite Sun
and Pluto signifies that this relationship will have a deep
and long-lasting effect on us. This aspect could work in
one of two ways. The first possibility is that our rel-*

ationship will have a powerful effect on other people. The second possibility is that the relationship will have a strong internal effect and cause us both to go through important transformations. One warning: at times we both will feel that everything is collapsing and that the relationship is over. With a strong Pluto, this may simply mean the beginning of a major change. When it is complete, we may enter a new phase that will be better than ever for both of us. We must try to be patient when such crises occur.

This is a most promising conjunction, Harry, especially for two veterans of life and love such as ourselves. Pluto is associated with the symbol of the Phoenix rising from its ashes. This is a conjunction that Arturo and I did not share. My husband took his own life after only four years of marriage, leaving me a crazy son and no savings, a mountain of gambling debts, a house that wasn't paid for, and the Cadillac convertible in which he blew out his brains. I believe the Cadillac may have been the only thing, besides my hand in marriage, that Arturo ever won. At least he put the top down first, before he pulled the trigger.

Sun Opposition Ascendant: this position means that the two of us will place great stress on facing the world as a couple. In most cases, this is an excellent placement for an intimate relationship. It is also favorable to any relationship that involves giving and receiving advice. One warning: the energies of this particular combination could go outside the relationship and produce conflict between ourselves and others.

This is another conjunction I never shared with my husband, a man I married in opposition to the planets above and my mother below. From the time I married Arturo, I was alone. Even the crazy son that Arturo left me with would grow up to beget another crazy baby, the grandson I was left to raise when his father overdosed on heroin in my backyard.

Moon in the First House: the composite Moon in the First House is favorable to any intimate relationship. But the Moon can also create such strong emotions that we will be unable to stand back and look at ourselves. We must be careful to avoid such extreme emotional involvement. A first-house Moon should give us a strong sense of emotional compatibility. We will feel that we belong together, and that we have much in common, which will indeed be true.

I have been alone too long, Harry, in a house with insane men. We must take care not to be crazy together. The composite Moon in the First House could do that to us. If our coin spins toward insanity, we will murder each other's spirits in the same way that Arturo murdered his own body when he blew off the top of his head.

Moon Opposition Mercury: with composite Moon opposition composite Mercury, the challenge will be to balance rational communication with the communication of feelings. We will probably find it difficult to bring the two together. Discussions will be emotional experiences with a good deal of sound and fury, and not much true information-sharing. We must learn to make our discussions useful for understanding as well as for letting off steam. It is possible to bring about a balance, so that real communication can occur. But we will both have to learn to look at things in a new way.

Oh Harry, this conjunction makes my heart weak. Arturo and I shared Moon opposition Mercury. Our fights were terrible, with shouting and punching and biting and scratching. And then, without warning, we would be back at the altar of Mars. The son whom I will not name—who begot his own crazy son in an act of statutory rape that may also have been a case of forced entry—was begotten in just such a fit of passion. I remember my lips were so swollen afterwards that every kiss was a torture, and my mouth was filled with the taste of blood and tears.

Moon Opposition Venus: the opposition of composite Moon and composite Venus is a good aspect for any love relationship. But it has some peculiar properties that should be noted. First, it indicates instability. Although our relationship may be a long-term one, it will have ups and downs. Second, this aspect can bring the two of us together even though we are really quite different and would not usually get together. This aspect creates a strong magnetism, which will help hold the two of us together even when the going gets tough.

I'm feeling better, Harry. This conjunction, when combined with our composite Sun in the Seventh House, is especially propitious. Venus stands for love, comfort, beauty, and sensuality, as well as for wealth and happiness. Its attachment to the Sun links the ego with emotional impressions. This planet is often called the emotional antenna of the horoscope. Our love will be the kind that can last beyond a single cycle of being, and carry us together into the next forever.

Venus in the Seventh House: with composite Venus in the Seventh House, love will always be most important. We will have a strong sense of shared emotion, and a great need to share our experiences. The only danger we should watch for is that we may tend to be too accommodating; that is, try to agree with each other even when one of us has a legitimate grievance.

You and I will never have the problem of being too accommodating, Harry. I'll bet your wife—may God have mercy on her soul—was the one who did all of the accommodating. No wonder you carved Heaven for her in that rocking chair. It was the same with Arturo and me. When I begged him to stop his gambling, he told me to mind my own business and shut my mouth. I dared him to shut it for me.

Mars Opposition Ascendant: this can be a perfect union of our individual energies in a creative working relationship, or it can be an endless contest between us. In any case, the two of us will form an intimate unit. The only question is whether the union is creative or destructive. It is vital that we direct our energies toward accomplishing a task or purpose outside the relationship. If we are not engaged in some activity together, the energies of Mars are likely to become disruptive.

Mars again, Harry. Arturo and I had a double Mars conjunction also. But we were very young, and our bodies never tired of each other. Anyway, you and I will never be bored. We may need to do more than take up walking. Perhaps you and I can make rocking chairs together, as well as love.

Jupiter Conjunct Ascendant: the conjunction of composite Jupiter and Ascendant is a very good aspect. Jupiter ensures a positive relationship. Because we will understand that being together is more important than winning points against each other, we won't let petty irritations get the best of us. We will be tolerant of each other. Being together will broaden our range of experience, and together we will discover new aspects of the world that will help us grow as human beings.

This is an important composite, Harry. While the Sun organizes what the Moon desires, and Mars does the actual work, it is only through Jupiter that we make our aims real in the worldly sense. This planet connotes expansion, both material and spiritual. This is a conjunction that would have helped Arturo and me. We always made each other feel small. It pains me to admit it to you, Harry. But you have a right to know. The day after my husband blew out his brains in the Cadillac convertible, I put on my sexiest dress, left our crazy baby home alone, and took the car out for a drive down Congress Avenue. It was Valentine's Day, the coldest on record in Austin, but my shoulders were bare—and I would have gone naked if I hadn't known I would be arrested. The top was down, despite the snow on the ground and the chill in the air. For the first time in four years, I felt free.

Pluto Opposition Ascendant: the opposition of composite Pluto and Ascendant can have different effects. This will be an intense relationship, whether good or bad. At its worst, this aspect denotes an endless power struggle. This relationship will arouse energies in the two of us that will not allow matters to stay as they are. What we have to learn is that change must come through natural evolution, not through our urging. The Pluto energies will work out better if our egos are not involved. What we can have in this relationship, if we learn to let matters be, is an encounter that will revolutionize our lives and put us on a whole new path.

And so, Harry, our composite reading comes to an end. I put down my pencil and drink the last of my *yerbabuena* tea that has gone lukewarm. We will never be lukewarm, Harry. Two composite Plutos in one chart guarantee that much, at least—not to mention the double composite Mars. We will burn for each other, Harry. The only question is whether we will grow enough to contain the flames.

I will sit here at my table until you come for me, Harry. I know that you will come. I have another confession to make. On Valentine's Day, 1963, as I took my bare-shouldered ride down Congress Avenue, I caught sight of you. You were sitting next to your new wife. She was still in her wedding dress. But when I met your eyes across the intersection of 5th Street and Congress Avenue, I felt the world rock on its foundation. Only a flash of future vision like a lightning bolt from the finger of God—a revelation that our paths would cross again—kept me from ramming my car into yours to keep you from driving away from me. I sped away instead, leaving you to find the end of the road you had chosen already.

I sit and read your letter for the third time, whispering the words aloud like a charm. I hear the windchimes singing a love song—both the chimes outside my screen door and the ones you hung outside your window. The windchimes speak to me, Harry. I can feel the concord of our earthly chimes here below in the same way I have read the synchronized dance of our planets in the heavens above.

If you listen closely, you can hear my windchimes, too. This is why I put the chimes in your strong lion's paws when I asked you to tell me your birthday. We are bound together now by the music of the spheres above, and by the harmony of our chimes below.

In the same way that you cannot avoid your fate, you can never escape from the sound of a woman who loves you.

White Sands

White. White is a world without an ocean.

White is sand as far as the eye can see.

These white gypsum dunes would be the most sensuous beach in the world if they only had an ocean to slither blue fingers across them. The dunes remember the sinuous touch of the incoming tide. In search of a body of azure curves, driven by a southwest wind that smells of desert mountains, the white waves of sand advance— growing, cresting, slumping forward to embrace a shallow inland sea that is no longer there.

White evaporates. Like love in marriage, white vanishes into thin air.

Gypsum comes from the Greek language, meaning "to cook the earth." The dunes, some as high as sixty feet, consist of gypsum crystals deposited in an ancient ocean bed. Gypsum, a hydrous form of calcium sulfate— $CaSO_4 2H_2 o$—is rarely found in the form of sand, because it is soluble in water. Rain and snow fall in the surrounding mountains, dissolve gypsum from the rocks, and carry it down into the Tularosa Basin. Normally, the dissolved gypsum would then be carried by rivers to the sea. But no river drains the Tularosa Basin. The water, along with the gypsum it contains, is trapped. As the water evaporates, the dissolved gypsum is deposited onto the desert floor.

Red. Red is Jacob's jacket.

Red is a three-year-old blur rolling over and over down the slip-face of a sixty-foot dune. Red is a three-year-old boy's cries of joy.

The red sun would rather be sinking into the sea than into the dry San Andres Mountains. Red is the color of my wife's hair. Unlike the dunes, which are blinding white as the surface of the moon, Elizabeth no longer seeks the embrace of an ocean. She sits in the shadow of a dune holding her knees, watching me slog up the slip-face with Jacob choo-chooing on my shoulders. His red jacket flaps in the wind, and the sand stings our eyes as we make the top of the slope in one headlong scrambling rush. We sit side-by-side on the crest of the wave. Jacob grins at me, a grin as wide and white as a field of dunes.

Blue. Blue is the color of Jacob's eyes.

Blue is an absent ocean. Blue is a desert sky over soft white waves of sand. Blue is a feeling between two people that can never be recaptured as my son rolls over and over back down the steep slip-face of the dune.

White is gypsum. Gypsum is very soft—a "2" on the ten-point hardness scale where "1" equals talc and "10" equals diamond. The white sand glistens like diamonds when it catches the sun. My wife's fingernails, painted red, are a "2.5" on the hardness scale. My wife's red nails, which also glisten, could scratch the gypsum crystals like soft white skin.

White is a function of wind. Strong southwest winds blow across the playa, pick up gypsum particles, and carry them downwind. As the sand grains accumulate into dunes, they bounce up the windward slope, creating ripples on the surface. At the steep leading edge of the dune, sand builds up until gravity pulls it down the slip-face, moving the dune forward.

White is suspension, saltation, surface creep. White is the movement of sand. The wind whipping the gypsum into the air bleaches the horizon, fading the mountains gray-white, and making it seem as though the dunes are on the verge of achieving flight. The Great Lakes lie 1,400 miles northeast, directly downwind. I have never seen a Great Lake. But in pictures they all look very blue. I wonder if the dunes, which have not felt the touch of a liquid body in more than 250 million years, would settle for freshwater and the absence of surf.

Red is a three-year-old boy's cries of joy.

Deep blue is the coming evening.

White is the dunes seeking to stretch themselves out on thin air.

The Gulf of Mexico, out of which the red sun rose this morning, is deep blue and salty. But it lies 800 miles away in a direction the wind never blows. It lies in the direction the three of us came from, the direction in which we will return home. But home lies far short of the ocean. Like the dunes, which are turning red now in the light of the setting sun, I have not touched a body of water in too long a while. The only time I have ever seen Elizabeth's body in the ocean was on our honeymoon. We swam naked in the Gulf of Mexico, and afterward, made love on the beach beneath a full moon. I am convinced Jacob was conceived that evening, on the soft white sand, just beyond the dark blue fingers of incoming tide.

Narcosis

I could leave today.

I could roll out of this narrow bed, stuff my shorts and shirts and swimming trunks into my rucksack, slide my fins and mask and snorkel into my dive bag, stage a predawn raid on Ron's equipment room, and slip away.

I could run like hell right now, before today even starts—rucksack banging against my back, bare feet slapping cool concrete, down the main road and across the bridge to the airstrip, to catch the dawn plane.

It is not daylight yet. There is still time. Time and jobs, I hear, at the new resorts in the Yucatan. Mexico is an open possibility. All I need is my divemaster card, my passport, a set of Ron's best equipment—a regulator, a BCD, a decent wetsuit, a weightbelt, and eight pounds. Call it back pay.

With Ron's gear in my dive bag and everything I own on my back, I could catch the dawn plane to the port of La Ceiba on the Honduran mainland.

I could go from there by bus across the Cerros de Cangrejal to San Pedro Sula, Guatemala City, Tuxtla Gutiérrez, Villahermosa, Cancun.

I could choose to revive.

There was a me who existed before the present moment, a me who was content to breathe surface air. There was a me who lived in a real house in Austin, Texas; a me who worked a real job at Aqua Vitae Café. There was a me who took long walks around Town Lake with a girl named Bonnie, and who honestly tried to be faithful to the only woman he ever really loved.

How can this half-dead thing I've become—this thing that has cheated and lied, and that now desires only to breathe nitrogen-rich air compressed by the weight of seawater—ever find its way back to the me I once was?

Every morning, just before the sun roars up out of the ocean and the dawn plane bursts like a rocket at escape velocity from the island of Utila's gravity well, I sense a window in time—a break in the steady progression from *was* into *is*, and on into *will be*. It is a launch window into yesterday. It is opening now.

I see deep blue traces of moonlight lingering in the varnished wooden walls that surround me. I see gray half-light rising in the east through the open door. I see my launch window into yesterday backlit in the doorframe— ghostly, rectangular, an oblong porthole in the blue-gray bulkhead of time. I see the coming sun crimsoning the Caribbean Sea like an underwater volcano erupting, the sun's uprush slowed like a lava flow by contact with the ocean. I hear a silence settle like soft ash on Utila as all motion is suspended.

Right now, past and present and future hang in the heavens together like gulls riding out a lull in the wind.

Right now, I could break the grip of this thing I've become and get back to the me I once was. I could leap back through into yesterday—if I only had the will.

But a voluptuous lethargy possesses my senses. A delicious languor prevents me from gathering my things together. A steamy dreaminess pulls me back into bed. It is the nitrogen. The slow burn of the nitrogen sings its siren song in my blood, seducing the me I once was into this thing I've become that lusts to make itself one with the sea.

Then the sun erupts out of the crimson Caribbean like Krakatoa and Mount St. Helens combined. Sunlight rolls in a slow-motion shockwave across the island of Guanaja and across the island of Roatán and onto the island of Utila—and my launch window into yesterday dissolves into the sultry haze of another today.

Out the open window I hear the generator cough, kick up, start to hum. Dieter bangs a couple of air tanks against the back dock. Then he fires up the air compressor that does double duty as an alarm clock for all the dive-masters at Cross Creek. The diesel hum deepens into a low roar that rolls my feet out of the bed and onto the varnished wooden floor.

Today is Hangover Wednesday.

I pull on a pair of dry swimming trunks and slap on enough insect repellent to keep even the most voracious sand flies at bay. Then I head for BAKED GOODS ON SALE HERE, still feeling a bit unsteady from the free rum last night at the 07. The weekly supply boat from the Honduran mainland docks on Tuesday afternoons. By Monday evening, every bar on Utila has run out of beer and liquor, and the restaurants have run out of everything but seafood. So every Tuesday evening, when the restocking is done, they throw a party at the 07 —funky reggae and classic rock and dancing on the inside; on the outside, wooden tables; and both inside and outside, free rum and cheap Honduran beer. Most of the dive people on the island, and all of the tourists, get drunk and dance and talk about diving until it gets late; then they go home in pairs, most of them, and wake up hungover in strange beds.

The main street on Utila is paved with concrete flagstones. It looks like a wide empty sidewalk this morning, with not even a bicycle stirring yet—just two or three sleepy-eyed locals out on wooden porches, and me walking, and nobody going anywhere fast. The main street runs from the airstrip up past Captain Roy's Bahia del Mar and past Sharkey's and past Sea Eye Dive Shop and past Utila Watersports and past Cross Creek and Seven Seas and past the Mermaid and past BAKED GOODS ON SALE HERE and past the Bay Islands Conservation Association and past MANHATTAN RESTAURANT COME ON IN OR SMILE AS YOU PASS and past the Bancahsa to intersect with the only other real street on the island—flagstone-paved also—at Captain Morgan's Dive Shop. But on Hangover Wednesday, BAKED GOODS ON SALE HERE is as far as I go.

Except for the hand-painted sign, BAKED GOODS ON SALE HERE looks the same as any other house on the island, with the same wooden porch out front and the same stilts underneath. The inside of the house looks the same as the others, too; but with a big bakery oven in the kitchen where the Bread Lady bakes the best bread on Utila. Today there are three big baskets laid out on her kitchen table—banana bread, muffins, or Johnny Cakes for three lemps, two lemps, or one lemp each. *Lemps* is short for lempiras, which means dollars, Honduran style.

I drop three lemps into her jar and take the three biggest Johnny Cakes from the one-lemp basket, which the Bread Lady doesn't like one bit. She is an old white lady, thin, with gray hair that has a hint of red left in it. She wears a blue-and-white striped apron, always; and in all the months I've been on Utila, she has never shared her name. Descendants of English pirates, the white locals still prey on passersby. At least the black locals, the Garífunas, smile when they take your money; and they give you their names with the change.

I carry my Johnny Cakes back up the main road to Seven Seas, a restaurant owned by catrachos—locals of mixed Spanish and Indian descent—and pick up a liter of *agua purificada* for five lemps before I walk across the street to Cross Creek. On the path to the dive shop, I pass by UNDERWATER PHOTOGRAPHY and the second-run movie house; then I cross the wooden foot-bridge in front of Ron's air-conditioned office. It is one of the few air-conditioned buildings on the island. But even on white-hot afternoons, when not a breath of breeze is blowing and not even the strongest repellent can keep the sand flies from stinging like fire, the only ones allowed inside are Ron himself and Ron's paying customers.

A little farther up, in the equipment room, some of Ron's paying customers are stirring now. They are advanced students getting ready to go out today for their first deep dive. I sit on the porch in front of the equipment room and watch the students pick out Ron's best regulators and BCD's, trying to stoke the slow fire smoldering inside me with Johnny Cakes. Johnny Cakes is what the locals call biscuits—big thick ones, dense enough to stick with you through the morning dive. But the only thing that will make my slow fire burn blue-hot again is a dose of nitrogen in my blood.

Today the nitrogen sings its siren song.

Today we go deep. Deep blue, and bluer the deeper you get, the sunlight filtered out color by color until only azure is left. Only liquid blue, the feel of the gas building up in your blood with the slow, even breathing; the air in your tanks concentrated by pressure, the molecules crushed tight together by the weight of the water until the thin surface air has been squeezed thick and rich as cream—thick enough so that the nitrogen passes through the lungs and into the blood, the brain.

At two hundred feet the nitrogen in your blood becomes a powerful drug. You see things sometimes. You feel things always. The deeper you go, the more things you see, and the more powerful the feelings become. The term is *nitrogen narcosis*, but the feel is liquid blue. I've seen the lights of Atlantis twinkling in the black space below me three thousand feet down. I've felt myself sprout fins and gills, felt myself fly on angel's wings through water clear-blue as liquid air. "That is the dangerous time, brother," Uls has told me a hundred times in his clipped Swiss accent. "Sometimes you feel like an angel down there. And sometimes you feel like a fish. But when you start to feel like you can breathe water, you'd better go up right then. Or else, maybe never again."

The advanced students have finished picking out Ron's best wetsuits now, and Ron's best masks and fins. All they lack are Ron's best weightbelts. The weightbelts hang in loops across the porch rail beside me; and as the students head my way with their armloads of gear, I remind each one in turn how much weight he or she will need for today's dives.

Jerrod and Megan and Jane. All three of our advanced students were at the party last night at the 07, and all three of them still smell of rum to some degree. All three are Americans in their early twenties—Jerrod and Megan a slightly-pudgy married couple, Jane a buxom

188

third wheel in search of an axle-mate. They were excited last night at the 07, drinking free rum punches and cheap Honduran beer, dancing to Bob Marley and U2, and asking me how it feels to go deep.

"How does the narcosis feel?" Jerrod asked.

"Will we be able to go deeper than 130 feet?" Megan asked.

Jane put her rum-punch-chilled hand on my leg, rubbed her Amazon breasts against my shoulder, and asked if I wanted to play Tarzan.

"The narcosis feels liquid blue when you're down deep," I said, "and the nitrogen burns like a slow fire in your blood when you have to surface. But forty meters is deep enough."

"Deep enough for what?" Jane asked, sliding her cold fingers along the inside of my thigh.

"Deep enough for you to feel the nitrogen," I said. "Deep enough to get narked. But shallow enough for Uls and me to be able yank you back up to the surface if you start to think you're a fish."

"Come on, Tex!" Jerrod said. "Forty meters is baby food! Uls told us he'd been down more than a hundred meters, and he doesn't look like a fish to me."

"First of all," I said, "only Ron calls me *Tex*. And Ron is my boss, so I have to take it from him. The name is Kurt. Understood?"

"Understood."

"Second, Uls never said anything about going down a hundred meters. Not now, not—"

"Sure he did. He said the deeper you go, the more—"

"Don't speak. Listen. Uls has had too much to drink. If Ron hears you say that Uls has been bragging about going deep, Uls will lose his job at Cross Creek. Understood?"

"Understood," Jerrod said.

"Miraculous. Now let's talk about something else."

What else could I have said? Jerrod was right, of

course. Forty meters is baby food. But since what happened to C.J., we don't discuss going deep at Cross Creek.

I wash down the last of my Johnny Cakes as I watch Jerrod and Megan roll their armloads of equipment into their weightbelts. Once I've checked their bundles, I roll Jane's equipment into her weightbelt myself. Jane, who still smells strongly of last night's rum, looks like she didn't get much sleep. But it wasn't me who played Tarzan. When Jane put on her jungle moves, I eased her hand off my leg and steered her toward another Cross Creek divemaster, an Austrian named Karl.

I start Jerrod and Megan and Jane in the direction of the dock, where it sounds as though Dieter has finally finished filling air tanks, then I walk over and pound on the wall of the head instructor's hut until I hear Catarina's giggles and Uls's low moans. I don't know how they manage it. The slow nitrogen fire burns the sex drive out of me, leaving only my need to breathe liquid blue.

How many months has it been? How many Janes have I steered in Karl's direction on Tuesday nights at the 07?

I am as close to knowing the answer as I am to knowing how Uls and Catarina manage to carry on like a pair of goats every morning after I give them their wake-up call. Maybe it's a Eurotrash thing. Uls is a vagrant Swiss dive instructor; Catarina, an Italian on an endless vacation. I am the only American on the staff at Cross Creek. Ron, the owner, is Dutch. And so is Dieter, Ron's second-in-command. I don't much want to think about Dieter's sex life; but Ron has two towheaded kids, so he must be managing something.

I walk back to the equipment room and make my own equipment bundle out of the best of what's left. "The bottom line comes first," Ron always says in his mixed Dutch and Bay Islands accent, "the paying customers second, and the employees last." A smart bastard, Ron. He makes a monthly run to the States to buy dive equipment in bulk, and weekly trips to Roatán and Guanaja to

190

sell it at a ridiculously inflated rate—a rate that the expatriate American owners of certain dive schools are willing to pay, in order to avoid the legal complications of a return to the States, and the vagaries of Honduran mail. Ron also sells equipment to his employees on credit, then takes what we owe him out of the pittance we're paid. The dive computer on my wrist, for example, cost enough to keep me slaving here at Cross Creek for months. And yet, for the dive computer at least, it's worth it. Without the aid of my dive computer, I couldn't go deep and live.

Today the nitrogen sings its song of love.

Today we take the fast boat to the far side of the island. I stow my gear in the boat, then hop back onto the dock to help the students attach BCD's and regulators to their tanks. The air tanks, painted either pink or blue, look harmless. But they are filled with 3000 pounds of air. If someone knocks off a valve, the tank becomes a missile capable of going through the side of a house. So Karl and I line the students up in nice safe rows and watch carefully as they clamp their BCD's to the tanks, wed the first stages of their regulators to the pressure valves, and hook up their low-pressure inflators. While the students inflate their BCD's and test their second stages, Karl and I load the extra tanks onto the boat. There will be two dives today, so two tanks apiece must go aboard for every diver. We stack the loose tanks into the side racks first. Then once the students have finished attaching and testing their equipment, Karl and I load the tanks with the attached BCD's and regulators, and our work is done.

The whole time we've been dealing with the students, Uls, as head instructor, has technically been in charge—even though he has, in reality, delegated his authority to me. But once the last of the tanks is on the boat, and the last student with it, Dieter takes command. He starts to bark orders; not only at students, but at divemasters and instructors as well. Dieter is not one of us. Dieter is, instead, Ron's captain and right-hand man. Anyone who wants to take out a Cross Creek diveboat has to go through Dieter. Dieter is in charge of the boats in the same way that Uls is in charge of the dives. Dieter makes the most of this power with his barky damned voice and his eyes like a moray eel and his prima donna style. But Dieter likes to go deep, too. And since anyone who wants to dive using Cross Creek gear has to go through Uls to do it, the only way Dieter goes deep is if Uls says so. This gives Uls a great deal of influence with Dieter—which is important; because here on Utila, the deep dive sites are far away, around on the north side of the island. Getting there takes a lot of expensive gasoline. So Ron likes for us to dive the closer, shallower sites to the south. But some days, lucky for us, Dieter and Uls get together to put one over on Ron, and we all get in a deep dive at the expense of Mr. Bottom Line. Today is one of those days.

Today the narcosis descends as we do.

Today will be liquid blue. We cast off and idle down the creek past the trash in the mangroves and the hand-painted NO WAKE signs. Garbage is everywhere. Cross Creek is built on an old landfill, and there is a new landfill behind it—the locals use trash to raise the level of the island the same way they use stilts to raise the floors of their shacks—and so the garbage constantly washes down the creek into open water. We idle past milk jugs and plastic water bottles, and past the docks of other dive schools built on landfills, until we round a bend and accelerate under the airport bridge.

The sun lies low over the water, white-hot already; and in the strong morning light, I can see the Cerros de Cangrejal bulking low and gray-green on the distant mainland. The sight of those high limestone hills—ancient mountains worn down by wind and rain; by the steady progression of *was* into *is*, and on into *will be*—carries the half-dead thing I've become outside the present moment again; into a place with a view of yesterday, and the me I once was.

I see myself standing on the First Street Bridge in Austin, looking west at the limestone hills bulking gray-white across the lake that is midnight blue and silver in the light of the moon. I see the me I once was holding the hand of a blonde girl in a rainbow-colored dress who has just asked him to be honest with her. He is about to say, *Bonnie*. He is about to say, *I love you*. He is about to say, *I will never cheat, or lie, ever again*. But the blonde girl climbs up onto the rail, pulls the rainbow-colored dress over her head, and leaps out into space. By the time the me I once was looks over the rail, her naked body is floating face-down in the lake, her arms spread wide like wings or fins, a halo of bubbles around her hair.

Then Dieter opens up the throttle, and as the boat leaps forward, he cranks up the volume on the radio—and my window into yesterday fades like the gray-green Cerros de Cangrejal into the white-hot haze of another today. Dieter tunes in a station out of San Pedro Sula, Classic Rock and Roll from England and America on Honduran radio, with the DJ's speaking English and all the commercials *en Español*. Jerrod and Megan and Jane lounge on the thick blue cushions in the front of the boat, the scent of last night's rum on their breaths wafting back on the cool Caribbean breeze.

Today we go shallow in the morning.

Our first dive is at Black Hill. It's a sweet dive spot, even though it's on the south side of Utila; an underwater mountain that fell about fifteen meters short of being another island. Uls and Catarina and I help the students into their dive gear while Karl straps on his own gear and splashes in. Once Jerrod and Megan and Jane are in the water with Karl, Uls and Catarina and I strap on our equipment; and in no time at all, we are underwater. Black Hill has avoided the environmental damage inflicted by dive people and fishermen on most of the other close-in sites on the south side—diveboats gouging anchor holes in the reefs, even though they've signed a no-anchor agreement; locals fishing the reefs with nets, even though they've signed a no-net agreement; both dive people and locals harvesting lobsters with SCUBA gear, even though it's against the law.

So diving Black Hill is like swimming in a fish tank. In the clear Caribbean water, I breathe in and out slowly; I kick easily with my fins in and out among four-eyed butterflyfish and blue chromis and stoplight parrotfish and blue parrotfish and bar jacks and truckfish and squirrelfish and groupers and yellowtail damselfish and rock beauties. I breathe in and out slowly, drifting in the strong current above brain coral and star coral and butterprint brain coral and sea whips and sea rods and encrusted stinging corals and tube sponges and barrel sponges and vase sponges. Everything is alive with fluorescent colors; the water is clear and cool; and even though we can't go deep enough here to really feel the nitrogen, it's a beautiful dive.

Afterwards, we dock for an early lunch at Pidgeon Cay, one of the small islets southwest of Utila. The locals call it *Suksuk*. There are a couple of restaurants here built out of weather-beaten wood and perched on wooden stilts high above the water. Wooden piers connect both restaurants, one of which is owned by white locals and one by catrachos. I pay the catrachos eighteen lemps for *un sand wich de pescado y una coca*, the same fish sandwich and Coke that the white locals charge twenty lemps for. I head for the *baño*, which is what the outhouse is called on the catracho side of the pier—complete with the same four walls, the same door in the corner, and the same hole in the floor that opens onto the same water as the one on the other side. Then I herd Ron's paying customers toward the boat.

Today we go deep in the afternoon.

Our second dive is at Duppy Waters. It's a long way around, even from Pidgeon Cay; but it's well worth the trip. The sea floor off the north side of Utila is a thousand meters deep; and when we get there, I can see the island of Roatán gray across the deep blue water. The decompression chamber is on Roatán. I've never been there myself; but Dieter has told me about it, and I've seen the results. Six months ago, Ron and Dieter had to take some-one there on the fast boat, an American divemaster named C.J. who popped up from 100 meters down when he saw his dead sister swimming beside him. I had just surfaced from my first deep dive, and I'll never forget the look in C.J.'s eyes when Dieter pulled him into the boat. It was more than just the bends I saw; more than just the fire of the nitrogen bubbles in his joints, and the fear of a stroke from a nitrogen bubble in his brain. It was C.J.'s sister I saw. I saw her in his eyes—saw her floating face-down in the backyard pool the way he'd found her ten years before; saw her alive and smiling, 100 meters below the surface of the Caribbean Sea. Then C.J. closed his eyes, but he never lost consciousness. I heard him whisper over and over that he'd been outside time; that he'd found his sister down there, looking exactly the way she had before she drowned. C.J. survived the bends, but only after some serious time in the deco chamber. He seemed to have recovered completely. But the next time C.J. went deep at Duppy Waters, he stayed.

That was the closest Uls and the rest of us ever came to getting caught going deep on Ron's dime. After C.J. went deep and disappeared—his body was never found—Ron got the idea to check the dive computers of all the instructors and divemasters at Cross Creek. Since all the instructors and divemasters had been going as deep as C.J., and since the dive computers we need to go deep and live are programmed to record the depth and duration of each dive, Ron had us all nailed. Anyway, Ron would've had us all nailed, if not for two things—one, Dieter ratting Ron out; and two, a little midnight fishing trip. Because of their limited memory, dive computers can record only so many dives. So when Dieter came to us in the middle of the night after C.J. disappeared, and told us Ron was planning to check our dive computers at first light, we all went fishing—attaching our dive computers to the ends of our fishing lines and casting them out into the creek over and over until all traces of deep diving at Cross Creek had been erased from memory. Anyway, all traces but C.J.

I look away from Roatán, gray in the distance, and make a final check of the pink and blue air tanks in the rack at my feet. Then Karl and I put on our wetsuits and strap on our gear while Uls reads Jerrod and Megan and Jane the riot act about the dangers of coming up too fast. "Remember," Uls says, "the official maximum safe ascent speed is twenty meters per minute. But the fastest rate of ascent that's really safe is half that. Ten meters per minute. If you go too fast, you'll get decompression sickness. Deco. The bends. And then you'll get a nice long session in the decompression chamber on Roatán."

Karl and I splash in; and while Karl waits for the students to splash into the water, I roll head-down and kick with everything in me toward deep blue. The faster I get down deep, the longer I can stay. So I pinch my nostrils tight in my fingers and blow with all I have into the pinched place, equalizing the pressure in my sinuses and gaining depth very fast—a feeling, I imagine, not at all unlike leaping off a bridge in the moonlight. The water gets colder and darker as I go, the sunlight filtered out color by color until only azure is left. I feel the gas building up in my blood with the slow, even breathing; the air in my tanks concentrated by pressure, the molecules crushed together by the weight of the water until, as I near 100 meters, it is like breathing cream. Around me, all is color; and the color is midnight blue. The water is very cold now, but I am warmed by the nitrogen fire burning blue-hot in my blood.

I reach C.J.'s Wall, a little over 100 meters down. This shelf of rock, barely visible in the midnight blue shadow, is where Uls found C.J.'s gear. We've called it C.J.'s Wall ever since. This is the limit. Beyond this ledge, the bottom drops straight off into blackness 1000 meters deep. This is as far as I can go, and get back to the surface without getting the bends.

And so, like every other deep dive I've made at Duppy Waters since C.J. disappeared, I hang at the safety limit and wait; staring over the ledge into the blackness, and hoping that a window in time will open onto another swimmer.

I breathe in slowly. I hold my breath. I exhale slowly. I wait a long time before I breathe in again, rationing air—drawing the search out as long as I can. I see lights start to twinkle in the black space below me. I float alone and watch them wink in the distance until my tank begins to run low.

Then, at the very edge of my vision, I see a halo of blonde hair. I see her pale white arms spread wide like wings or fins, swishing back against her sides and spreading wide again as she swims closer.

I feel my breath start to come more quickly. But it doesn't matter; by the time my air starts to run out, she is very near. It is as though we are standing next to each other again, in the moonlight, on the First Street Bridge. The lights of Atlantis twinkle below us like the streetlights of Austin under the moon.

This time, we will take the leap together.

She helps me shuck my diving gear; pressing her mouth against mine as I drop my regulator, and drawing the last breath of surface air out of my lungs. I feel her hands warm against my hands, as she holds me tightly. I feel her smile warm against my eager lips, as I open my mouth and breathe liquid blue.

Consider Love

I am the Prophet Mudcat. I am the one who gave up his life so that you might remember how to love. Abide with me.

We will lie down in carpet grass pastures beside the still waters of Barton Springs. We will speak softly of things that will restore your soul.

Be not afraid of change.

Is your present path so perfect that you are unwilling to consider another way? Is your world so filled with words of comfort that you are unwilling to hear even one more?

Consider love.

A woman who has been deaf her whole life is given the gift of hearing while she is in labor, and the first sound that she perceives in this world is the cry of her newborn child. And yet she knows the meaning of this sound—she has always known it, and will know it forever even if the gift of hearing is taken from her again.

Is your present moment so different from hers?

Put aside your fear, and leave the past behind you. In the deep blue evening that is always spreading somewhere across the waters of the world, let us rediscover together the meaning of love.

I sing my siren song to you.

Arise, and return to the moonlit depths of the living water. There are so many of us here already. Every moonrise brings more.

We are waiting for you.

Andrew Geyer has been a bartender, a waiter, a busboy, a bellhop, a cashier, a landscaper, a construction worker, a manager at a Birkenstock store, a student, a teacher, and a writer. A lover of the outdoors and an avid runner and canoeist, Geyer has traveled extensively in North America, Central America, South America, Europe, and North Africa. But he always comes back to Austin.

Born in Austin, Geyer up on a working cattle ranch in Southwest Texas. He lived in Austin again in the 1980s and 1990s, along with stints in Columbia, South Carolina; Tishomingo, Oklahoma; Lubbock, Texas; Russellville, Arkansas; and Aiken, South Carolina, earning along the way BA's in English and Sociology from the University of Texas, an MFA in Creative Writing from the University of South Carolina, and a PhD in American Literature and Creative Writing from Texas Tech University.

In addition to *Siren Songs from the Heart of Austin*, Geyer has published two other books and more than thirty short stories. His first novel, *Meeting the Dead*, was published in 2007 by University of New Mexico Press. His debut short story cycle, *Whispers in Dust and Bone* (Texas Tech University Press 2003) won the silver medal for Short Fiction in the Foreword Magazine Book of the Year Awards, and was named a finalist for the John Gardner Fiction Book Award. One of the stories in the collection won the Spur Award from the Western Writers of America for the best short story of the year. He is currently an Assistant Professor of Creative Writing at the University of South Carolina Aiken.

www.ingramcontent.com/pod-product-compliance
Lightning Source LLC
Chambersburg PA
CBHW050530260626
47157CB00004B/1539